Wings & Other Things

WINGS&
OTHER
THINGS

STORIES

CHAUNA CRAIG

Press 53

Winston-Salem

Press 53, LLC
PO Box 30314
Winston-Salem, NC 27130

First Edition

Cover art "Heart tree stock illustration"
copyright © 2022 by Vizerskaya, licensed
with permission through iStock.

Cover design by Claire V. Foxx

Author photograph by Hannah Colen

Library of Congress Control Number
2022937789

ISBN 978-1-950413-51-5

To the women who give me wings and keep me aloft, and to those who help me land safely. You know who you are.

The author is grateful to the editors of the following journals and publications in which these stories previously appeared, sometimes in slightly different form:

Crab Orchard Review, "To Taste"

Elsewhere Lit, "Smoke, Iowa"

Fugue, "Scrap Moon"

Mountains Piled upon Mountains: Appalachian Nature Writing in the Anthropocene (West Virginia University Press), "Wings and Other Things"

People Holding, "Scorcher, 1979"

Phoebe, "Big Sky Blue"

Prairie Schooner, "Harm's Way"

Pretty Owl Poetry, "Teresa of Pierce County, Nebraska"

ROAR: A Journal of the Literary Arts by Women, "Impossible Blue"

SmokeLong Quarterly, "She Waits between Slug and Egg"

Sou'wester, "Controlled Burn"

CONTENTS

Impossible Blue   1

How the Rainforest Buries Its Dead   13

The Empty Set   19

She Waits between Slug and Egg   35

The Ferry Man's Smile   39

Harm's Way   49

Teresa of Pierce County, Nebraska   67

Scorcher, 1979   69

Controlled Burn   73

Scrap Moon   83

Smoke, Iowa   93

The Sweet and the Heat   97

Parting Gifts   113

To Taste   119

Wings and Other Things   123

Big Sky Blue   133

Author Biography   151

Acknowledgments   153

IMPOSSIBLE BLUE

She always saw him between worlds, when the only certain thing she could say about her life was *in transition*. He'd appeared at her apartment door the same week in May she'd dropped out of her second college. He was driving across country from Portland, Oregon, to Philadelphia to see an old girlfriend. "You were on the way," he said, an intense grin spreading his thin face. Bozeman, Montana, was not on the way, not if you wanted to get somewhere, and a secret thrill pinched her stomach.

Later, after Thai food at a new restaurant rumored to be owned by occultists, they drove up Hyalite Canyon and sat by the lake to watch the moon. It rose yellow as honey, hardened to a silvery pearl as the hours passed. They huddled, arms around each other, the way they had in his dorm room that first year at the private college she'd failed out of, after they'd tried to analyze each other's dreams for psychology class and, once, the possibility of past lives.

On that past-life night, candles flickering on his desk
and windowsill, she'd fallen into a deep meditation,
listening to the soothing voice on his mother's new age
tapes, imagining she was pulling right out of her body,
up through the dorm, floating. When she lighted down,
she saw herself in chains, weighted to the ground, bent
in supplication. After the tape had snapped off, after
they'd cuddled up—their only physical intimacy—to
watch the wax drip, she'd said aloud that she was once
somebody's slave.

"Yikes," he said, shifting his weight away from her.
Flustered, she said she had to study for a biology test,
then spent the evening walking alone through the tiny
town's empty streets, daring the dogs to bark at her.

Once, before the end of the school year, he'd kissed
her in a wheat field where they'd gone to study the stars
for an astronomy final. A single, lingering kiss. She felt
herself rise out of her body, just for a moment. And
then she transferred in-state, failing out again before
the summer constellations returned to the sky.

As they huddled under those same stars, he asked,
"How happy are you?"

That's how he was, assuming the best and wanting
only to hear of its intensity. "Happy," she said. "You?"

He shivered when the spring wind launched off
the lake. "This life treats me well. I must have figured
something out in the last one."

"Do you really believe in past lives?" she asked, thinking again of their last kiss and the whispering wheat stalks.

"Maybe not literally," he answered after careful
consideration. "But I believe in the past and how it can
seem like a life that's no longer yours."

"Wow."

"Yes." He laughed. "I'm so utterly profound." *Yes,*
she thought, *you are.*

He dropped her at her apartment with a warm,
brotherly hug, thanking her for their moonlit talk. He had
a motel room and an early start planned. She unlocked

the door to the empty kitchen, aching, watching the tile floor wash white with the streetlight, then recede like the tide when she shut the door.

The next time they met, she had her business degree and a hospital job that sent her to conferences like the one in Portland—*Health Care and Public Image in the Electronic Age*—that she skipped to go hiking along the coast with him.

He seemed taller and thinner, a six-foot reed bent into a waterproof jacket. And he had a trim beard. But he hugged the same, as full and warm as skinny arms can manage.

They had breakfast first, plate-sized pancakes and coffee that burned her tongue. She remembered his letters after that moonlit visit, in which he pondered chaos theory and the New Age, telling her how they each had multiple lives running at the same time, that every decision made took the present life one direction, the possible life onto some other, now impossible plane.

"Do you still wonder about the lives you didn't live?" she asked.

His face scrunched into a frown as his mind searched. He knitted his fingers together, and a thin band of gold flashed a warning.

"How every choice erases one life and opens another?" she prompted, sure she was quoting the letter. She'd read it that many times.

"Oh that." He laughed. "I used to think all kinds of things."

She glanced into her coffee cup and saw that it was nearly empty. She waved at the waitress for a refill, changed her mind. There were no bathrooms on the trails he'd choose.

The trees were dense and lush green at the base of the trail, a wet, glimmering canopy like something in a fairy tale. Wrapped in the second waterproof jacket he'd been smart enough to bring, she labored up the path behind him, trying to disguise her ragged breath. The trail wasn't so steep, and her lack of endurance disgusted her. He talked, asking questions, carrying the pack with their lunch, his camera, and a hidden bottle of wine, and she grunted her replies, stopping occasionally to feign interest in some plant or re-tie her bootlaces while she calmed her breath. By the time the trees thinned and the sky opened wide and blue, her skin was tacky and damp. She couldn't be sure if she smelled the salt of the ocean just beyond the hill or her own sweat.

"Close your eyes," he commanded, stopping suddenly to cover her face with his large hand. She smelled him then, soap and musk, a smell she could inhale until her lungs collapsed. She let him walk her slowly up and up to the crest of the hill before he took away his hand.

Eyes closed, she felt the ache of that night in Bozeman. She held on to that tight hurt in her chest a moment before exhaling and opening her eyes.

"Sweet Jesus." She whispered the words, and the ache came back in wide, rolling waves in rhythm with the blue ocean she saw from this mountainside. Miles of rolling water stretching back to where the misty clouds swallowed it, stretching forward in a steady series of waves to the rocky shore where the white surf pounded and slid back. She heard it a beat after she saw it. *Shh-thum. Shh-thum.* Like a watery heart. They stood in fractured sunlight.

"I knew you'd like it." He stood off to the side, coat flapping in the strong wind. That grin. For a moment, a splurge of a moment, she imagined this was heaven, he the gatekeeper who'd just unlocked her apartment door, revealing a whole rushing world of water, sky, and diving gulls, asking her to take that last step over the threshold.

"Yes," she said. He knelt to open his backpack and she saw him down on one knee. "Yes," she said again, then remembered the ring he already wore. He pulled out a plastic sack of sandwiches and a small blanket to lay on the damp grass, and she felt silly and young, like he'd evolved into a man while she'd reverted to the college freshman who'd embarrassed herself claiming to be a slave.

They ate lunch and tasted the wine before deciding it was too sweet. He stopped another couple hiking past and asked them to take a photo, so she nestled into his chest with the whole ocean behind her, windblown hair in her face, and said "cheese."

Later, when he sent a copy, she'd see that her eyes were closed, that even if she'd opened them, she'd have been looking in the wrong direction.

After that embrace, they didn't let go. He thanked the couple and took the camera in one hand, keeping the other pressed against her back. They sat again, and he said he was cold, so she moved closer. They talked about people they knew—Jonas from the dorm, who'd hanged himself the year after she left; Rhonda, her old roommate, pregnant with her third—and then his lips were on hers, more open and pressing harder than the time before. Everything amplified: the whisper of wheat now the roar of an ocean.

She kissed back, sliding into the taste of the sweet wine on his tongue and the salt of his lips. The beard scratched at her chin and she thought suddenly of Albert.

"I've been seeing someone," she said, pulling away, stunned at how bright the sun blazed now.

"Oh? Anyone I know?" he joked, the weight of his arm on her shoulder.

"Albert. He's an optometrist."

"How happy are you?"

"In which life?"

She watched from their vantage point high on the cliff as a group of teenagers chased each other on the rocky beach below. She remembered a trip a group of them had taken that first spring at her first college, a month before he'd kissed her. Camping at Palouse Falls, where she'd sat alone at the top, watching the fierce tumble of water, wondering what it would feel like to fall and fall and fall. She remembered now that he hadn't been there, but Jonas had been. Always playing "Let It Be" on his guitar, he must have known on some intuitive level that it was the last spring of his life.

"In the optometrist life," he answered.

She thought about Albert with his prickly beard and old-fashioned name, how they'd been together three-and-a-half months and he already imagined how their children might look, how he could sit in a room so quietly that she almost forgot he was there. How she liked that.

"Happy," she said. "And he keeps my vision 20/20." It was like a prophecy, saying that. She peered out in the surf with his arm still carefully curled around her shoulder, and she gasped, really seeing for once. "Look, whales." She pointed, and then he saw them too, killer whales playing in the surf, glimpses of their shiny black tops cresting the waves, spouting plumes of white water.

They held each other then, reverent, watching the whales as darker mist rolled in off the ocean, and a family of four hiked by and advised them of gray whales further out.

Why, I bet they think we're lovers, she thought as he dug for binoculars in that pack, nearly knocking over the re-corked wine. Would Albert think so if he saw them? Would Albert say this was cheating? She didn't have to think long. Of course he would. Just the holding part would strike him as intimate, which it was, and unfair to the children upon whom he'd already imagined his own features. But this was merely another life, a past life she revisited from time to time. The kiss was cheating, something stolen from her present life, but the warmth of another body and the gift of whales—they were hers to hold on to, to cork like that sweet wine and tuck away.

She'd told Albert about him, her friend from the first college. She'd mentioned that she'd get to see him, but she hadn't told Albert about skipping the conference or how, even when she'd first boarded the plane, her heart had raced with expectation. Albert called him Out There, referring to Portland and the West Coast but mostly to the stories she'd told of their dream therapy and past lives regression. "That's out there," Albert had laughed, and the name had stuck.

"I don't see any grays," he said, handing her the binoculars, "but you're the one with the 20/20 happy life today."

She looked, trying to find something through the lenses, but no luck. She even lost track of the orca in the surf.

"Are you seeing anyone?" she asked finally.

"You're right in my line of vision." His eyes were warm, searching. He expected her to respond in like, with something witty that would fan the small flame she felt in her belly. She could see in a flash what would happen, that they might not wait for a hotel room but roll in the surf of their own bodies here on this mountain. The flame rose inside her. She felt like the melting wax dripping on the windowsill all those years ago.

"So you're still single."

It was mere statement, flat and without wit, and he expelled a soft sigh. "Looks like it," he agreed, smiling, letting his arm drop to his side. A blade of cool air cut between them, surprising her with a shiver, and she saw him cloak his ringed hand in his coat pocket.

On the flight home, she wished she'd seen the gray whales migrating, sure that, if she had, she'd feel fulfilled, wouldn't have this warm yawning sensation in her belly, this stretching desire with no real object. She wanted something, something *more*, and as she crunched the fragile ice cubes in her plastic cup, she resolved to break up with Albert.

He was waiting with a small bouquet of wildflowers, his beard in desperate need of trimming. He hugged and kissed her and asked what she'd learned about her public image in the electronic age.

"It's shaky," she said. "The picture's always breaking up. You can't tell what's real."

Albert laughed. "You sound like you've been Out There."

"I saw him. He's a marketing manager now."

Another merry laugh, a real gut laugh that charmed her the way it rooted her to that very spot in the airport terminal. "That's what happened to all those new age guys that every woman wanted. VW and TM turned to pure collar-and-tie MBA."

"He never had a VW," she scoffed. "And you need to shave that beard before you start to look like one of those guys."

She and a clean-shaven Albert married the next year. Her invitation Out There was returned to sender, address unknown, and it wasn't until she'd had her first baby, a scrawny, colicky thing she loved with parts of her heart she never knew she had, that she heard anything about him. Her old roommate, Rhonda, called to congratulate her and catch up on gossip about the friends they had in common, who, after only a year together at college, were few. Of course his name came up. Rhonda said she'd heard he was on the East Coast with his wife now.

"I didn't know he was married," she said, trying to sound casual.

"Ooh, girl. That's a story." With relish, Rhonda told how his wife was schizophrenic, had been hospitalized more than once, and spent most of their marriage living with her parents instead of him. "It's sad," she conceded. "But I always thought she was weird."

"You knew her?"

"She lived on our floor. You don't remember Kenna Clay?"

She couldn't recall someone with that unusual name, not even when Rhonda described her as stick-thin and pale with short black hair and permanent circles under her eyes. Who could forget a ghost like that?

"How long have they been married?"

"Since the end of college I think. Quite a while. I'm surprised you didn't know, but now that I think about it, they eloped, and nobody really kept in touch with him."

The baby started to cry from the other room, where Albert was watching him, and her nipples tingled and started to leak.

"Did they ever live in Philadelphia?"

"Could be? I wouldn't know," Rhonda said. "Some big city."

She nursed her baby when she hung up the phone, feeling the pull of milk like a tide. She held the baby closer, unable to imagine her life as real before this, before she was this body, this mammal mother with so much to give—blood, milk, the waters that had spilled from her. Still, she felt the warmth of his body for a moment, the snugness, the protection of an imagined life. She held her baby even closer.

After the second child, a girl, she found the photograph. The two of them on a cliff in Oregon, the sea an impossible blue. His grin, her squint-shut eyes. The perfect second when the shutter stopped the universe, freezing the fierce wind in a swirl of her curls, the sharp flap of their coats, the motionless chop of the waves.

She tried to find him again, but Rhonda was right— no one had kept in touch with him, and his name was so ordinary that every attempt led to thousands of possibilities as though he were all of them, split by a million decisions into a million people, none the right one. She tried the college alumni association, a dozen search engines and email directories. His name gave her passage to nowhere, and she realized with growing despair that the trail was cold and choked over with weeds.

She began to stare at photographs. The Oregon one and the ones around the house, wedding pictures, family portraits. She mostly studied her own face. Saw it was composed of bits and pieces, fragments sewn expertly together, even the very molecules, which she knew from basic physics were held together by atoms. Infinite pieces in an accidental combination she called herself.

There was no her. Or maybe there were millions of her and she just hadn't discovered the right one.

When Albert found her early one morning, wide-eyed and staring at the pictures in the hall, ghastly circles under her eyes, her skin pale as something unearthed from under a rock, he sent her to a doctor.

When the doctor suggested she go back through her life, looking for the "root," for the first time she felt failure, she laughed. "In which life?"

"In this one of course." His brow wrinkled as if he were calculating something very complex.

"Doctor," she said calmly. "In this life I'm a terrific success." And she went home to her husband, her beautiful children, and let that life be her life until, only a few months later, Albert was killed while jogging, hit by a driver who'd made the simple, irreversible choice to grope for a dropped pen.

After the funeral, her parents told her to take a trip, leave the children with them, and just get away. They meant a cruise or resort, some place she could be pampered, put color back in her mourner's cheeks. No one understood why she bought a plane ticket to rainy Oregon. But it was her grief, so they let her go with wishes for health and relaxation.

She rented a car in Portland, stopping to buy a map when she realized she knew only that the coast was west. She drove that direction, leaving the interstate. She looked for the diner with the plate-sized pancakes, finding only winding roads that split into forks every few miles. And each time, she would pull the car off the road and sit and wait until some voice in her head—some life that was no longer hers—told her which way to go.

She ate up the afternoon and half a tank of gas that way. By the time the sun set, she'd seen the coast but nothing that she remembered. She knew she was seeking a place she couldn't drive straight to, but still, it all looked strange. The voices led her at last to a small motel with a lit vacancy sign. She didn't drive at night, and besides, what could she find in the dark where everything bled together?

She slept with her window open, cool mid-summer breeze curling in, bringing with it a strong smell of the briny ocean. She was too late for the gray whales, the clerk told her with a shrug. Timing was everything.

She slept in ragged patches. Albert visited her dreams, wearing his wedding tuxedo and offering her glasses of wine. In her dream, she kept shaking her head no, not that one, not sweet enough. And still he brought more. In the morning, she craved sugar and snatched a donut from the lobby. Then, feeling guilty, she wrapped it in a napkin for later.

She drove again, her desperation rising with the slow sun. Nothing looked right. Everything was amphibious green, warm, damp, cool, shivering between worlds. She pulled off the road to cry, and the first tear started a flood. She cried and cried, all of her selves pitying, sympathizing, grieving, complaining, shedding. When through the open window she smelled that strong salty breeze, she followed it, driving red-eyed to a wide stretch of public beach. She tucked the donut in her pocket, the one where she'd secreted the old photograph, and walked purposefully down to the water's edge.

The tide spurted over her shoes, a foamy mix of broken shells and seaweed. She kicked off her shoes and began to walk south along the water's edge, letting her footprints wash away behind her, pausing sometimes to look back and know they'd disappeared. A jogger and his dog passed by, neither paying her any attention, and she stared after them. Then she walked faster, dropping her jacket on the sand when she got too hot. Sea birds squawked at her as she rounded a small bend and began to climb the slippery rocks that ringed a cave where the tide smashed splendidly, then echoed a second, lonelier sound. Soon she was wet from the spray, but she stayed, staring out at the brilliant blue ocean, imagining there may yet be whales, those few that lagged behind, their sense of timing disrupted by age, infirmity, or some other distress.

She took the photograph from her pocket and brushed sugar grains from it. She held it tightly, studying it piece by piece: his neat beard, the wildflower her foot hovered near as if deciding whether to crush it. She'd never noticed that before, the way one foot was just above the ground, threatening a purple blossom. She compared the blue of that water to the sea before it, realizing with a small hole of sorrow that she'd carried a fake ocean for years. The one before her was ten times more blue, and frameless.

When the salt spray began to dissolve the photo, opening pinpricks in the image, the colors intensified and threatened to bleed. She put the picture back in her pocket, wrapping it in the grease-stained napkin and throwing the donut to the curious gull behind her.

"What do women do these days?" she asked the gull. It hopped back instinctively. "They don't just walk into the sea anymore, do they?" The photograph wasn't enough weight to hold her down anyway. It wasn't an anchor or even a link of iron chain.

She lay back on the wet rock, listening to the roar of the ocean, inhaling its birthing smell over and over again. Some shade of herself swam out looking for whales. She felt it rise and slip out while she stared at the cliffs above. She wondered if any hikers stood up there, peering down at her. Would they think she was a woman who'd fallen and broken something? Or an ancient mermaid who'd finally remembered which half of her was home?

HOW THE RAINFOREST BURIES ITS DEAD

In the rainforest, her wool coat was a burden. Plum-colored, painting her bright as the tropical birds that flitted so close, stirring her hair. The coat weighed her down, made her sweat in the climate-controlled mugginess of the zoo's rainforest. When she complained, he carried it.

Theirs had been a tentative courtship, each making advances that could be interpreted as simple kindnesses. He offered a ride home from the bookstore where they worked; she brought him a croissant when he couldn't take a break from inventory. One night he kept driving, past her apartment, into his own driveway. He offered wine and the companionship she'd longed for since her divorce.

This was their first escape together from work and the holiday season. He'd surprised her by driving to the zoo in Omaha, remembering that she'd never been. He remembered everything; she was careful what she said.

"Better?" He folded the coat over his arm. He'd checked his coat, shivering between buildings in order to be comfortable inside. She'd worried the fluctuating temperatures would aggravate her cold.

"I can carry it myself. Really." She reached out her hand, and he caught it, pressing his lips to her fingers.

"I insist," he said, "that you worry about spotting those little yellow monkeys I told you about. Lyddie loves them." He smiled and let her hand drop.

She glanced down from the walkway that snaked through the building, through Southeast Asia, Africa, South America. She didn't know which continent she was currently visiting, and the birds—soaring across borders, glibly ignoring where they were supposed to stay—irritated her. She felt her nose start to drip. Her tissue packet was in her coat pocket. Her coat was in his arms. And he was on the other side of the walk, staring into a leaf-plastered pool. She approached, rubbing at her nose with the back of her hand. Before she could wipe her hand on her blue jeans, he reached for it.

"Come along. I have to get Lyddie by five." Lydia was his daughter, the only thing his wife had left behind when she'd run off to Texas with a dental supply salesman.

She drew back, holding her hand behind her, and he reacted as if snubbed, wearing a perplexed, possibly angry, expression. They'd never argued about anything except where to go for lunch, so she wasn't sure. Her ex-husband she could read before his facial muscles twitched.

"What was that?" he asked.

"What?" She tried to slowly, inconspicuously wipe her hand on her pants. A monkey howled from somewhere over her shoulder.

"Your reaction when I mentioned Lyddie. You practically recoiled." His voice was fiercely steady.

"No," she stammered, "I just—"

She couldn't explain that she didn't want to get snot on his hand. But she couldn't let him think she didn't like his child. He talked about her all the time: how cute she looked in her Big Bird jammies, how smart the preschool instructors thought she was, how much she missed her mother, who called weekly and sent new Disney Princess toothbrushes every three months.

The Lydia talk did get tedious, but she would never say that aloud. She had no children, no clue what it was like to be consumed by parenthood. She glanced at the coat bunched under his arm and wished she'd never relinquished it.

"Maybe you're just tired?" he offered. He circled an arm around her and rubbed her shoulder. His fingers were remarkably strong, his touch hypnotic. She sank under his touch. With her ex-husband, she could never relax. Thin and all bony angles, his body had never fit with hers, their embraces awkward. This man was larger, softer, his pillowy middle a place she liked to nuzzle and press the way a kitten weaned too soon will knead anything soft. All that softness—she feared being swallowed into it.

"Not too tired to finish our world tour. What's in the pool?"

"Nothing you want to see."

She broke free of his hold and strode over to the railing. Scanning the top of the leaf-plastered water, she wasn't sure what she was looking for until she saw it.

There, among the waxy green leaves, protruded the stiff tail feathers and wings of a scarlet bird. The head, buried below the surface, wasn't visible. Its black-fringed wings were spread as if frozen in flight, buoyed by floating leaves.

She stared, mesmerized by the brilliant contrast of red and green on the gently rocking water. She thought of the Christmas decorations she still hadn't packed away.

"You're not upset?" He hovered at her side as though she were fragile, fingers poised to massage her anxieties away.

"Upset? I didn't even know the deceased." She was disturbed, just not sure why.

"I just thought . . . that mouse incident. You're sensitive."

"Mouse incident?"

"The pet shop. The snake?"

She remembered the anecdote she'd told about visiting a pet shop with her ex-husband when they were first married. They'd been looking for a pet, probably a cat, to fill that nuclear family urge without the expense of diapers and daycare, and he'd called her over to the cage of a small boa constrictor.

"Check this out," he'd said, pointing to the corner of the glass terrarium. There, huddled under an artificial plant, was a hairless baby mouse. Its eyes weren't open yet, and she swore it was shivering. The snake paused to assess the threat of its audience, then returned its predatory gaze to the mouse, and she'd bolted from the shop. Her then-husband found her sobbing on the sidewalk, drawing stares from downtown shoppers. Such a dramatic, embarrassing response. She was surprised she'd told this story, even more surprised to remember, now, the ending: her ex-husband had held her until her tears dried.

"You've got quite a memory," she stated, looking back to the red bird's tail feathers. The leaves fanned under the body were so shiny she wondered if they were fake.

"Memory is a gift," he whispered. He pressed his body into hers, becoming amorous while the monkeys howled from another continent.

"So is forgetting," she said. But she was mostly envious. He memorized scenes down to their scrap details, reminding her a week after some romantic tryst what had been playing on the radio. She was losing pieces of her ex-husband's face, of the body she'd known intimately for almost five years. Was the birthmark he'd always called his "extra nipple" on the left side or right? She tried to remember her fingers tracing it, but both sides seemed wrong. She wondered how the rest of the women remembered it, the ones who had lingered over her husband's body those weeks she traveled to Kansas or Missouri for her job with a college textbook company. She'd taken the job at the bookstore—too late—to save her marriage.

She turned from the water, checked the time. "Your daughter's waiting."

The fierce patience of children. She imagined Lydia: breathing clouds across the daycare's front window. Tracing lopsided hearts and stars in the fog, furiously wiping them away. Then starting all over again.

THE EMPTY SET

They said they hired me because I knew what I was getting into, but what did I know of keeping— grounds or house? Just that we're all always trying to keep something in or out of our lives. At Desert Heights Residential Support Community, the residents struggled every day to expel addiction and hang on to hope. The newest ones were all terrified—of using, of not using, of each other, of themselves, of the dim and confusing underground corridors that connected all the buildings. Rainn, the purple-haired poet, liked to tell new arrivals that those halls were haunted by a ghost named Gracie.

"Listen," she explained on my first day, when she thought I was there to dry out. "Back when this was a psych hospital, Gracie was a patient, beautiful and young but so sad all the time. Her sadness tunneled down into her core until she thought the sadness *was* her. So she was afraid to let it go. But this new doctor came, a psychiatrist with fresh tricks like hypnosis, experimental drugs. And Gracie's jealous lover, an orderly at the hospital, asked her to meet him at the stairwell—that one, there by our library. Then he strangled her!"

"Why?" I interrupted.

"Why what?"

"Why was he jealous of the doctor?"

Rainn heaved an impatient sigh. "The doctor doesn't matter. Gracie's lover didn't want her to get better because then she'd leave."

"How do *you* know all this?" I asked. The psych hospital had been two iterations ago for this institution that sprawled over several acres like a college campus or country estate. Red brick buildings with stately trees ringing an open area of green, cultivated lawn in a desert climate, where robins, thin and dull, searched for worms. First an army fort, then a military hospital that specialized in treating tuberculosis, followed by a psychiatric hospital, a state prison, and now a state-supported transitional community where people with alcohol addiction could dry out and find jobs, permanent homes, better lives.

Rainn narrowed her eyes, shuttered with thick strokes of eyeliner. "I channel ghosts," she declared. "If you were one of us, you'd understand."

During my interview, the director asked what I understood about substance abuse. "I realize this job is about keeping the place clean and looking good," he said, "but you'll be spending your day interacting with all of us, residents included, and I have to know that you can be comfortable with a wide range of behaviors." Dale went to church with my mother, and though I resented everything he already knew about me, I played along.

"Well," I answered, "I know—because my drunk father almost killed my mother—that 'substance abuse' means that a person who's never had a drop of alcohol herself might end up needing a full-time job right out of high school so she can be home to help her mom get into bed at night and out in the morning, at least until her father gets out of jail and we can pretend everything is back to normal."

Dale had heard it all; part of his job was to listen to the same story with its endless variations. He simply nodded, this man who always wore button-up shirts, shiny shoes, and a solemn navy tie to remind the residents that he wasn't their buddy, that he had the power to send them back to the streets.

"Recovery is a long journey—" he began.

"And life is like a box of chocolates. Look, I do want to give this job a try," I said. "I can clean up messes. I can be nice to everybody." I held his gaze until he nodded.

Desert Heights was, of course, in the desert, three miles from my tiny town and three hours by car from the crowded city streets where many of the residents had once spread their sleeping bags. *Five* hours away for those who violated the drug and alcohol policy and were escorted onto the next meandering Greyhound bus with whatever they could take in a duffel bag. When the place first opened, my mother referred to it as "Temptation in the Desert," complaining that taxpayer money was wasted to bring addicts together in the middle of nowhere. "They're just moving their problems," she said, referring to the state's capital city, "dumping the burden on rural areas as usual." By the time she was urging me to apply to work there, she'd changed her tune, even used the phrase "sacred mission," though she had never stepped on the grounds and never would.

One framed poster in the entryway of the administration building, where every new resident underwent a lengthy process of assessment and intake, read, "Recovery is a process, not an event." Another read, "Life is a marathon—you're in it for the long haul." I hated that second one especially, resisting the athletic metaphor, resenting the lie. A boy in my tenth-grade class had sprinted to his suicide, and my mother could only wheel herself on her life's "long haul" because of how the car crumpled. Her lower spine was crushed but not her lungs or her skull or her strong heart. My father bruised his shoulder, got a couple stitches above the eye, the scar disappearing into his bushy brow.

I did basic housekeeping and maintenance tasks in the office and common areas, day hours like the office staff; a company from a town twenty miles away sent people a couple nights a week for deeper cleaning—floor waxing, carpet shampoos. I liked to tuck in my earbuds, choose a playlist to suit my mood, and focus on simple repetitive tasks like running a vacuum over the same strip of carpet until it stood a little higher and looked nearly new.

"You still alive in there?" Eddie, a veteran who wore his army jacket every day, even over his pajamas, always asked that when he had to tap my arm to get my attention.

"Are you?"

The first time I'd responded that way, Eddie's face, usually set to safe neutral, reacted with surprise. My mother would have told me to cut the sass, but Eddie closed his eyes and pressed three fingers to his chest, sliding them up closer to his whiskered throat before pausing in meditative silence. Then he opened his eyes, dropped his hand, and said, "Seems I am. But my sister, she got shot dead by a cop six months ago. What about you?"

"Sure," I said. Then, "Sorry about your sister."

He shrugged. "Something you get used to in my community."

Later, I looked up the name he'd given and found the news article online and then the obituary, no mention of Eddie among the surviving family. When I confronted him with that, he told me I had a limited idea of family. I wondered if he was right or if he'd lied to me, or if maybe both were true.

But that became our ritual greeting and response—
You still alive? Are you? I found it comforting that
someone was making sure. After Eddie discovered how
much I hated the inspirational recovery posters hanging
throughout the building, even in the bathrooms, he would
sneak up on me and quote one. "The best preparation for
the future is to live as if there were none," he whispered
as I watered the plants in the waiting area.

"No way. That is *not* a real poster. Not in this place."
He shrugged and repeated *as if there were none* in an
ominous tone before inviting me to share his lunch table.
When I sat down beside him with a tray of macaroni
and cheese and shredded lettuce that passed for salad, he
told me, "Seriously, though, you should prepare for the
future. There's going to be a race war in this country."

I rolled my eyes, thinking he was just mouthing off,
but he insisted that I listen, that he wasn't joking. He
said he'd been all over the world in the military, that
he'd even killed men in other countries who he thought
of as brothers, and nowhere, he said, was as racist as
America. "And I'm telling you because I like you, and
you're young, and maybe you can protect yourself or
maybe not, but there's real vitriol between people, and
no president Black like me, or a white lady like you, can
smooth it over, and that's the most pressing problem of
the future." He stared into my eyes then added with a
hint of contempt in his voice, "Much bigger than every-
day alcoholism."

All day as I wiped spiderwebs from windowsills and
poured bleach in toilets I'd bleached the day before,
I thought about Eddie's prophecy—a race war in this
country—and I wondered why he was bothering with
this addiction support community full of people of all
backgrounds if the only future he could imagine had
them tearing each other to bloody shreds.

On my break, I wandered the warren of underground
halls to the basement game room and the little resident-
run coffee shop where I saw Rainn at a café table hold-

ing a card at arm's length, angling it to the light, trying
to read someone's handwriting. I paid my dollar and
took a sip of the strong and bitter store-brand coffee
brewed by the women who'd pooled their money for
this adult version of a lemonade stand. I asked Rainn
who sent her mail. Someone in the hall around the
corner whistled the chorus from an outdated, vapid
pop song that I knew would repeat in my head the rest
of the afternoon. I imagined for a moment that it was
ghostly Gracie channeling what passed for love in the
afterlife.

"Birthday card from my daughter," Rainn said, handing it to me. Thick and scratchy cardstock, homemade
with textured glitter in the shape of a shooting star.
The odor of cigarette smoke and something floral but
artificial, like air freshener, wafted up from the paper.
Written in marker on the front: "It's easy to boldly go
where no man has gone before." Inside, the punch line
was "Just be a mom." Her daughter had added a smiley
sticker, signing in exaggerated, looping cursive, "I will
always love you, Tina."

"I miss her," Rainn said, taking the card back and
tucking it under her notebook, where I imagined she
wrote poems or interpreted dreams or drew sketches
for the beaded necklaces she made in order to, as she
worded it, "keep the mind from thoughts of the bottle."

"How old is she?" I asked, trying for polite interest
as I watched the wall clock devour my break.

"Thirty-two." When my eyes widened in surprise,
she told me that she'd had the card for over twenty
years, that it had traveled with her to homeless shelters,
to new boyfriends' houses, to ex-boyfriends' houses, to
prison, and to rehab.

"It's not even my birthday. I'm a Scorpio. I just carry
this around and pull it out those moments I need it most."

I didn't ask why she needed it in that moment,
though later I wished I had. Instead I told Rainn what
I hadn't even told Eddie, how my dad was finishing his

sentence for a DUI, and he'd be back home soon. Thirty days to be exact, I realized, though I didn't say that aloud. I'd watched residents get their thirty-day chips at Monday morning meetings that everyone, including staff, attended. They grinned and pumped their fists in the air as they took the tokens from Dale's fingers, victorious in the moment while I watched, thinking how they were a single sip, a single slip, away from crashing. I imagined a cartoon sign, outside the gates of a factory, resetting when that happened, flipping backwards until it read "zero days without an accident." The zero would be pierced with a diagonal line like a spear through the heart. The slashed zero glyph, my math teacher liked to call that. The empty set.

Rainn smiled a faraway smile, one of those goofy, dreamy smiles I sometimes interpret as wise and meaningful when it's often mere vacancy. "I wondered why you chose to work here."

"It has nothing to do with that," I snapped. "You try to find a job in a dying desert town of 800 people."

"I just might do that," she answered, twirling the ends of her ponytail, more lavender than purple now. I saw the chalk line of gray growing in around her temples where her hairstyle couldn't hide it. "Can't imagine it's a good idea for me to head back to the city with all that temptation and past baggage. I'm supposed to be transitioning out of here. Stayed longer than most anybody's been allowed. But I really don't know where else to go."

I tossed the paper cup with its gritty coffee dregs in the garbage, careful not to splash on the wall since I'd be the one to clean it up. There, above the trash can, was the poster of an eagle and an inspirational slogan attributed to General Patton: "I don't measure a man's success by how high he climbs but by how high he bounces when he hits bottom." But how, General Patton, do you measure a woman's success?

I asked Rainn where her daughter lived, wondering if she might go there.

"I wish I knew, honey. But she didn't wait around for me to finally become the mom she needed." She paused and twisted her mouth into a wry smile. "Hell, she'd still be waiting."

My mom had a casserole ready when I got home from work that night. We had an agreement: she would cook if I set all the pantry ingredients on the card table where she could park her wheelchair at a comfortable height and peel and chop, measure and mix. Then I would clean up the kitchen and we'd watch Netflix until one of us started to nod off. Her queen-sized bed sat higher than most, the mattress even with my waist, and when I was younger, I called it the Royal Bed and told her she should put drapery around it for the servants to pull back in the morning. (She'd laughed in those days at the idea of someone serving her.) Although she could manage her own nighttime routine in the remodeled bathroom, she couldn't get into her own bed. I tried to convince her to buy something different, but she refused. Neither of us admitted this had anything to do with my father, how they'd shared that bed once and would again.

I ate my mom's casserole, mostly cheese and pasta, a richer version of the cafeteria's mac and cheese. I thought of Eddie's warning that the future was nothing but bloodshed and then about Rainn, who seemed unable to envision her future at all. At least I knew why my own future was blurry, suspended just beyond the frame of my imagination. I didn't apply to colleges or move to the city to look for work because I was waiting to make sure my father came home. Then I'd be waiting to make sure he kept alcohol out of his life, and his love for my mother in it. But *recovery is a process, not an event*. When were processes finally over? How long would I wait to "make sure"? At least *life is a marathon* gave hope of an ending. However long it took, that journey was still only 26.2 miles.

I helped myself to seconds, filled a kettle for after-dinner tea, and told my mom about Eddie. "He thinks there will be a race war."

"You should report him."

"For thinking?"

"For terroristic threats. For scaring people."

"Mom, he only said it to me."

"That's even worse! Harassing a teenager on her job. You should tell Dale."

I exhaled forcefully so the fake Gerber daisy in its bud vase trembled. "I wasn't scared. We have this thing, Eddie and me. No, I don't mean we have a *thing* in that sense. We just have this way of greeting each other every day where he'll say, *You still alive?* And I answer—"

My mother scraped her fork over her plate so sharply that I sat up, my spine straightening instinctively. When she spoke, she barely moved her mouth. "He tells you there will be a race war then asks you every day if you're still alive? How is that not threatening?"

"It's not like that. Just, never mind."

"Never mind? Now I'm worried. Maybe *I* should tell Dale and you should look for another job somewhere safer."

I whisked her plate away, though I could see she wasn't done, and I cleared our glasses and cutlery. I started the flame under the kettle, set out mugs, and moved with a brisk and brittle efficiency that, after a full day of work, I couldn't maintain. I collapsed back into my chair and looked my mother in the eye.

"Where I work, nobody drinks. Nobody gets behind the wheel of a car with a belly full of whiskey and misses a turn in the road." I saw my mother's face, stricken, then tightening. "Should I go on? Or just remind you that the only place safer than where I work might be, well, a prison?"

If she could have stood and reached across the table, my mother would have slapped me. I would have welcomed it. Instead, her white cheeks flushed as

I watched her struggle for calm. Finally, she exhaled a few controlled breaths and said, "I want to visit him this weekend, and I want you to take me."

"You know I can't do that." I shrugged and the kettle began its crescendo into shrill panic.

"You mean you *won't*."

"I mean that I know Ellen is happy to take you, and I'm happy to have her do it. Why mess that up?" Ellen was my mother's friend, the one she called when I was at work, the one who always answered.

"You work in a place where people walk up and threaten your life, but you can't go see your dad in a place where everyone, even good people like your father, is locked behind bars? What are you so afraid of?"

The kettle screamed for attention, and I filled our cups so the tea bags buoyed up, then bobbled in the swirling water before, saturated, they gently sank back down.

"There's nothing to be afraid of," I said, and I remembered a Sunday school class when my teacher had quoted Jesus on the water: *Be not afraid.* Only I'd heard it as *Be knot-a-frayed.* I'd envisioned a cleat hitch holding a boat in port during a storm as the tinier threads of the knot rubbed and snapped. And though I was later disappointed to see the ordinary phrase written in the Bible, I understood that my concept meant the same thing, only better: the world would wear on me, but I would not unravel.

I wasn't afraid my father would intentionally hurt my mother; even chained to my own stubborn anger, I knew he wasn't a violent man. I wasn't afraid he'd get behind the wheel drunk again. He sent raw, rambling, handwritten letters through my mother, all of them punctuated with regret and apologies and the repeated assertion that he'd never meant to hurt me, though I wasn't the one confined to a wheelchair. He claimed, and I believed him, that he'd rather be six feet under than drive with even a drop of liquor in his blood. Never once did he declare he would stop drinking though, and

I respected that he did not make promises he did not intend to keep. But who, I wondered, did he imagine would drive?

"The only thing we have to fear is fear itself," I told my mother as I tucked the covers around her later that night.

"FDR," she said, like we were playing a trivia game, match the quote to the speaker.

"The best preparation for the future is to live as if there were none," I suggested.

"Khrushchev? Kim Jong-un? Someone with a nuclear weapon and a bad attitude."

I laughed and kissed her good night, thinking how I wouldn't do this when my father came home, how it would again, after two long years, be their room, their bed, their nighttime ritual.

The next morning, I saw a green work order in my mailbox—a move-out, unexpected. Though part of the shared responsibilities for residents was cleaning their own dormitories, including a rotating list of tasks for both the bathroom and community kitchenette, I was in charge of cleaning vacated rooms. The Total Clean Out was a housekeeping priority because Desert Heights had a long waiting list. Also, cruel as it seems, as soon as possible they wanted to erase that resident's connection to the physical space they'd occupied. It helped with the grieving process, the counselors said, though when a resident was sent on the bus back to the city, their friends initially snubbed the person assigned to that room, as though the new occupant were to blame. Also part of the grieving process, the counselors explained.

That day's work slip was marked with a circle and crossed stem below, identifying the dorm as female, which meant I could go over without an escort. I signed out the room key and tapped in my ear buds, listening to some retro funk to wake myself as I navigated the underground shortcut to Building 8, the women's dormitory. When I matched the number on the slip to the number on the door, I assumed someone had made a mistake. The rainbow label taped to the door read "Rainn-bow!"

I found Laurel, the resident counselor whose office was just down the hall, in early, brewing a personal-sized pot of coffee and nodding rhythmically to her new age music: gentle drumming, trilling flutes. "Hey," I said, "I was assigned a TCO, but they wrote the wrong room number."

Laurel rearranged the pens on her desk, head down. "Room 22."

"But that's Rainn's room."

"I know." She looked up then, her eyes a shine of swimming tears.

"Is she okay?"

Laurel faked a smile. "I put her on the early bus myself."

"That's not what I asked."

"Is anyone okay?"

"I'm fine, thanks," I spat, rage cinching my chest over her flip non-answer. Later I would remember that she'd known Rainn longer than I had and that Laurel took all of the residents' failures on as her own. Less than a year later, she moved out of state to work in a private hospital.

I cleaned out the room, ignoring the other residents slowly walking past, pretending they weren't looking. There wasn't much to see. The room was stark except for some beads scattered along the baseboards, and a map of the city still tacked to her bulletin board. I saw inked x's and lines that must have meant something to her, but I took the map down and pressed it deep in the trash. I pocketed one of the lost beads—an egg-shaped amber swirl.

When later that day Eddie asked, "You still alive in there?" I answered without looking at him.

"Fuck off."

"Whoa, little sister," he exclaimed, hands up like I'd pulled a weapon. "Watch that mouth. No reason to get aggressive."

"No reason not to. There's a race war coming, remember?"

He chuckled and shook his head. "And you think your mouth is gonna save you. More likely get you killed."

"Are you threatening me?"

I jammed my hand in my pocket and rubbed Rainn's lost bead while I glared at him. I thought how I could plant a bottle in his room, leave an anonymous tip, show him he wasn't as smart as he thought. And then I felt like the petty, angry child I saw reflected in Eddie's expression, but I didn't break eye contact.

"Is this about the ghost lady?"

"Who?"

"You know, the lady always talking about ghosts. Purple hair. She got the free bus ticket last night."

I shrugged, pretending I had no idea what he was talking about. But the back of my throat itched, warning of tears. I couldn't remember the last time I cried, and so I blinked rapidly, willing it away. How many days without a meltdown? I could picture the sign flipping backwards, the big, fat zero of my heart with a slash through it. *Be knot-a-frayed.*

Eddie broke eye contact with me and I sensed it was intentional, respect for my grief. He didn't look back as he shuffled away in that oversized army jacket, and my tears slipped free.

"Sometimes," he called over his shoulder, "you got to think about all the pretty necklaces someone made and not their one wrong turn."

Ellen came through, faithful as ever, on the weekend my mother wanted to visit my father. She parked her car on the street, gave me her usual big hug and broad, crooked smile, and plucked the van keys from the wall hook to go lower the platform for my mother's chair.

"You can come with us," my mother said as she fiddled with the earrings she almost never wore. Her lips were stained bright as strawberries. I'd curled her hair for her, though she'd complained that she could do her own hair, thank you, and I said it was my pleasure, and you're welcome. She'd tried to suppress her smile and ended up with lipstick-mottled teeth.

"I have things to do here, Mom."

"*Things to do*," she scoffed, but then Ellen pushed through the screen door and called, "Let's hurry up and beat the traffic!" The two-lane highway was mostly deserted once you passed the Walmart and the intersection where one road veered north toward the state capital. Ellen made her little joke every time, and my mother responded with a quip about a prairie dog stampede. Sometimes jackrabbits, and once she switched it up to rattlesnakes.

"Good lord," Ellen added. "First clean those teeth. You look like a vampire fresh from a feast." She held out a tissue, and my mother rubbed her front teeth and peered at the pink tissue.

"Looks nothing like blood. You color blind?"

They were like an old married couple sometimes, bickering and finishing each other's sentences, and I wondered what might happen to these rituals when my father returned. My one close high school friend, Jennie, had broken up with her Neanderthal boyfriend not long after my dad was sentenced. We were inseparable then: late summer afternoons swimming and sunbathing at the reservoir, local division-nothing football games that we told ourselves we went to in order to mock the cheerleaders, late-night texting about celebrities and music so neither of us really felt alone. Then the Neanderthal left flowers at her house several days in a row, handwritten notes about what a fool he'd been, and finally a tiny opal promise ring strung onto the ribbon around a teddy bear's neck. When I rolled my eyes and said, "What a cliché!" Jennie's back went rigid, and her jaw clenched as she practically hissed the words that snapped the spine of our friendship. "I think it's *adorable*."

She became a cheerleader and rode to school in the Neanderthal's truck, pressed against him like a lizard warming its blood on a hot rock. He joined the navy when we graduated, and you'd think in a town our size I'd have known Jennie's every move, but I never saw her, didn't even hear if she'd stayed.

Would my mother become Ellen's Jennie? And why did I care?

"Mom," I said. "Next month. I'll drive." She didn't look back as she navigated the ramp, and I wondered if she'd heard.

I set to work as soon as the van pulled around the corner. Outside my mother's bedroom I lined up the duster on its extending pole and the vacuum cleaner with its various attachments. I set out furniture polish and unmatched socks for dusting, industrial glass cleaner and a paper towel roll, even my old toothbrush for the crevices. I tied back my hair and tackled the dust and dirt frantically, furiously. Total Clean Out.

I wiped down every surface, buffing the chrome trim on the nightstand free of fingerprints so it gleamed. Every stiff petal of the plastic, dollar-store roses my mother kept in a cut-crystal vase shuddered under the toothbrush's massage as the bristles loosened dust collected in the deepest coil of the corollas. I wiped the bristles on white paper towels that I buried in the trash like evidence. I picked up every crumpled tissue fallen too far under the bed, and I vacuumed in quick strokes until my shoulder ached, my scalp tingling with the first flush of sweat. I ran over the same trampled spots of carpet again and again, like I did at work, willing the frayed ends to stand a little higher.

I stepped back into the hall to study my work from afar. In less than ninety minutes, I'd cleaned everything.

Except that nothing in the room—not the yellow paisley comforter folded back in anticipation of clean sheets, or those scrubbed roses, still plastic and fooling no one— looked fresh or new.

I held up my old toothbrush, the nylon ends dingy and crushed. I studied the room again and noted with pride the shiny glass protecting the faded family photo taken on my first birthday (my mother's face pinched as she held me in mid-squirm), and the polish to the small cedar box where my father kept cufflinks he never wore. I weighed what I'd taken—layers of shed skin, the smudges of leftover touch—against what I'd left: my own invisible DNA and the illusion of clean.

I threw the toothbrush away and searched my sweatshirt pockets until I found Rainn's glass bead, its rich yellow swirl like amber preserving nothing. I polished the bead with the soft fleece of my sweatshirt and carried it to my parents' room, where I wandered, hovering over the roses, pausing at the foot of the bed, searching. I opened the cedar box and nestled the bead next to those shiny, useless cufflinks. But I couldn't close the lid and abandon this pretty thing to darkness. I picked up the bead, still warm from my hand. I held it to the light where it glowed, then closed my fingers around it, certain I'd find a place it belonged.

SHE WAITS BETWEEN SLUG AND EGG

In the refrigerator: two brown eggs. The farmer warned of blood spots in the yolk. Now she can't crack them.

On the porch: an enormous slug, luminous trail winking wherever the sun outwits the trees.

Inside on a stunning day. Snappish and hungry with a stocked pantry.

When the ex-husband calls, she responds: *Splendid vacation! No rain, fresh produce, a bottle of wine every night.* She doesn't tell how an owl attacked her or that the scratch on her scalp hurts less than her lover's words before he left three days ago. She says, "May I speak to my son?"

She waits between slug and egg, in a chair facing a wall.

Her son's no talker, but she keeps to the routine call. He knows enough words to consume thick paperback fantasies, never enough to reveal his inner life. Sometimes she fears that he, like his father, doesn't have one. More, that hers stopped developing and she noticed far too late. If someone cracks her open, look—a great bloody spot.

"Tell me something about yourself," she says, "something I don't already know."

"I've got hair on my toes. And I don't have a middle name."

"Yes, you do. My last name."

"Exactly. A *last* name."

"Then get rid of it. Like the toe hair. Shave off whatever you don't want. So yesterday," she tries again, "I saw a snow-capped mountain across the bay. Only it turned out to be a cloud."

"Clouds move. Mountains don't."

"It was a beautiful illusion while it lasted." She'd once believed slug slime was fairy dust.

"Mom, what's the difference between a neurotic and a psychotic?"

"Why?"

"Say you don't know."

"I don't."

"A neurotic imagines mountains that don't exist. A psychotic climbs them."

"Jokes are supposed to be *funny*. When the psychotic reaches the top, he pulls out an assault rifle to pick off all those people who don't believe in his mountain."

"Mom."

"You know how I get when my blood sugar drops."

"Bitchy."

"So I've been told."

"Dad and I are off to shoot hoops before dark."

"You'll be back in another month. Six more phone calls. Six more things I don't know about you—besides hairy toes."

"I'm sorry about Phil."

"What?"

"He called me yesterday."

"He *called* you?"

"Said he's sorry he won't be around."

"Does your father know? Never mind. Tell him I don't know the difference between a mountain and a cloud. He'll get a kick out of it."

"You don't really want me to tell him that."

"No, sweetheart, I don't." She hears crows fussing, wonders if the owl is back. "Think of five more things."

"Six."

"I didn't know you and Phil had exchanged numbers. So, five."

Those two brown eggs remain in the refrigerator, each concealing a small, cold heart. She doesn't have to crack them to know. By now the slug, more cloud than mountain, will be gone.

THE FERRY MAN'S SMILE

A man on the ferry thanked me for my beautiful smile." The two women leaned back in deck chairs, posed on the porch of a small bayside cottage, an open bottle of wine on the low table. "He said it just like that. 'Thank you for your beautiful smile!'"

"Did he ask for your number?"

"No. Why?"

"Nobody says something like that without an ulterior motive."

"You don't think I have a beautiful smile?" Melanie took a drink of her wine, scrunched her freckled nose. "This is awful."

"I warned you. *Loganberry* wine. Might as well be a wine cooler, us back at our first college party." Camille stared to where the waves broke, her hand wrapped fiercely around the glass from which she still hadn't drunk.

"Visitors Weekend. Pike Fraternity costume mixer. That was a great party."

"You passed out, Mel. You don't remember."

"Fair enough. Back to my smile then."

"It's beautiful. Sweet and open. But that makes you vulnerable. The ferry man wanted to fuck you." Camille swigged her wine. She made a gagging sound. "Ugh, remind me never to punctuate with dessert wine."

"I'm beginning to think this trip was a mistake."

"I *knew* it was a mistake when we booked, but we're best friends, Mel, and you need me. So here I am enjoying the first clear evening on the Island of Rain and Shitty Local Wine. I am here, dear friend, for you."

"You're the one going through the divorce. This trip was to make *you* feel better."

"Then get me better wine. And baby seals. You promised baby seals."

"I did not promise them. I only said it was the season."

"To everything (turn, turn) there is a season," Camille sang in the clear and lovely voice that had landed her a role in every school musical.

Melanie had stuck with yearbook, nurturing a talent for laying out cliché photos next to cliché captions, something she'd continued with her firstborn's scrap-book until she couldn't bear to paste down another exclamation point. Suddenly nothing seemed that important, and the last scrap she'd stuck in was a note that read, *See Memory Cards C1, C2, C3.*

"Fluffy white baby seals. That's what I want." Camille continued humming the song, softly speaking the *turn*s.

"The seals are in Ebey Bay."

"And we are in Useless Bay." Her laugh was bitter. "Excellent choice."

"I used my pin money to rent this place. It's what I could afford."

"*Pin* money?"

"It's something my grandmother said. I don't know what it means. Look, we'll drive to the seals tomorrow."

"Let's do it now."

"I told Tim I'd call him tonight."

"Oh. Checking in."

"I am *not* checking in. I miss him and the girls." She stopped. Camille had just lost in her divorce two adorable stepdaughters, playmates of Melanie's girls.

"Pin money. Sometimes you're so . . . quaint."

They watched two dirty, rumpled seagulls on the upper beach scrapping over something tasty in a shell until a dog galloped upon them. The birds hopped back, their wings half open, ready to flap away or beat something. They squawked their avian rage as the dog sniffed their prize, then carried it away in his mouth.

Camille swirled the loganberry wine and held the glass to the late evening sun to watch the pale red legs run down. She smiled. "Do you remember my costume at that party?"

"The Pike party? Weren't you the Grim Reaper?"

"You really don't remember anything from that night! That was *your* costume."

"Somebody went as Death in a black hood—that's all I remember. So what were you?"

"I wore a cute little black slip and carried a cigar."

"Groucho Marx? Grouchette?"

"No, I was a *Freudian slip*. Much cooler than those naughty nurse outfits that are all the rage these days."

Melanie was sure she'd seen a movie years earlier in which a character attended a costume party as a Freudian slip. She was also sure that in high school Camille didn't even know who Freud was.

"Sorry. I don't remember."

"Would you let your girls wear one of those naughty nurse or dead cheerleader costumes?"

"They're eleven and nine."

"That's when it starts. The road to slutsville."

"Camille!"

"I wasn't implying anything about your daughters, Mel. Just the culture."

"I need to call home now."

"Then I'm going to the tavern for a real drink."

Camille carried her glass of wine into the cottage, where she poured it down the kitchen drain, put on a light silk sweater, and after one last face check in the scalloped mirror in the entryway, grabbed her clutch bag and exited.

"I don't know what you expected." Tim sounded tired, naturally. It was late, and he wasn't on vacation. "Her husband slept with her younger sister. She's punishing you instead. Displaced anger."

"Since when did you have a PhD in psychology?"

"Since you worked overtime so I could finish that dissertation, for which I am eternally grateful and in your debt."

She smiled and pressed the phone closer to her ear. "What do you know about Freudian slips?"

"I studied the behavior of cocaine-addicted rats, honey, not psychoanalysis."

"I want to kill her. What do you think of that behavior?"

"That's not a behavior. That's a wish. And I'd advise against fulfilling it. I'd advise against cocaine too. It made the rats terribly anxious."

"I knew your expertise would come to some good. What if I said I want to *fucking* kill her? Is that Freudian?"

"Definitely. And I'd advise against that too. Seriously, be patient with her. I've never been Camille's biggest fan, but she's had a tough year."

By one o'clock in the morning, Camille hadn't returned, and when Melanie went to lock the cottage door, she noticed the keys to the rental car were missing, but the cottage keys still hung on the hook. Leave it unlocked? Lock her out and be wakened an hour later by the knocking? *You're so quaint, Mel. So open and vulnerable.*

She twisted the dead bolt to the left and turned off the porch light.

The hammering that awakened her sent her heart slamming high in her chest. Once she was past the fright and realized it was only the door-knocking she'd already predicted, fear tightened into anger. She fumbled to put on her glasses, then climbed down from the loft in her bare feet, flipped on the porch light, and twisted the dead bolt the other way. Swinging wide the heavy wooden door, she stopped short when she saw not Camille but a large man in khaki shorts and a designer sweater. Not your usual scary suspect in the dark night, but she was aware of her insubstantial cotton nightgown and her nipples erect in the cool wind, indecent.

"Tim!" She called loudly over her shoulder, pretending she wasn't alone and undefended, without even the mace canister she'd removed from her key ring before the flight out.

"Hey, shhh. I'm only here to get Cami's stuff."

"Cami?"

"Oh shit, have I got the wrong place?"

"Are you talking about Camille?"

"Maybe? Tall blonde woman in a coral sundress?"

"With polish on her toenails to match. We had pedicures this afternoon."

A man who could name the color "coral" was not likely a danger to anything but her fashion insecurity. Yet. "She can get her own stuff in the morning."

Melanie slammed the door and locked it as fast as she could. Then she scrambled up the ladder to the loft and sat in the center of the bed, clutching her cell phone in case the man knocked again or tried a window or who knew what. She couldn't stop shaking and slept poorly, bolting awake when a dog barked or the wind howled through the chimney. Finally, around first morning light, she called Tim on the phone that hadn't left her side and told him what had happened.

"Wait," he said. "She sent a strange man to your cottage in the middle of the night while you were sleeping?"

Melanie nodded, then remembered he couldn't see her. She tried to form a syllable, but her husband's words wakened her to the full realization of what could have happened, and she cried instead.

"Now *I* want to fucking kill her. Mel? It's okay. Nothing happened, honey. You're safe. Just come home. Is Camille there? Put her on the phone."

"I haven't seen her yet," Melanie said. "There's only three days left. I'll have a talk with her."

"A talk? That won't do any good. You need to come home."

"Tim, I've got it under control. Really. I love you. Thank you."

"Mel?"

"What?"

"Don't open the door anymore, okay? Not at night. Now I'm going to be worried sick."

She hung up, feeling she'd brought Tim into a ridiculous drama that was nothing more than typical Camille. And really, nothing had happened.

She made a pot of coffee and pulled on a sweatshirt to sit on the back porch where the bottle of loganberry wine still waited, uncorked, dewy, and sprouting a lump that turned out to be a small banana slug.

"Eww." She kicked the bottle off the deck, set her coffee mug down, then thought better of that and cradled it in her hands. Slug slime.

She was rising for a refill when Camille came around the side of the house and up the stairs to the porch.

"Are we going to see the baby seals today?" she asked, stretching and yawning.

"Why? So you have something else to club?"

"What the fuck, Mel? Good morning to you too." Camille looked terrible in the light of morning, her skin papery with foundation creasing her wrinkles, her hair a nest, her eyes bloodshot like she hadn't slept.

"We need to talk."

"Yeah, we do. I don't appreciate being locked out in the middle of the night."

"You sent a strange man to the door. I was afraid!"

"Of Billy?" Camille laughed. "He's a California surfer all grown up. Well, mostly grown up. He's harmless."

"Neither of us knows that. You put me at risk."

Camille raised a brow in disdain. "At . . . *risk*," she echoed. "Grow up, Mel. This isn't a frat party."

"Exactly! I could have been robbed or . . . something worse!"

"Raped?" Camille rolled her eyes and sighed. She looked out at the water, squinting. Mel pulled the sweatshirt tighter around her, noticed she'd sloshed her coffee on it, a dark stain that she would forget until it had already set. "Do you remember Marty Barker?" Camille asked then.

"What does he have to do with anything?" Marty had been a year older. A loud-mouth, muscled, state champion wrestler, someone she avoided in the halls because he always tried to brush her breasts with his hand. His graduation was her freedom.

"He was at that party. He told me he wanted to fuck Death. It's like he was asking my permission or something."

"So you did it. Congratulations."

Camille's lips twisted into a peculiar smile and she stretched up and back as if preparing for yoga, a sun salutation. Then she vigorously twisted back and forth. "I wasn't the one dressed like Death." She rolled her neck and shoulders. She squinted across the bay again. "Too hazy to see Seattle. Useless Useless Bay!" She smiled and shrugged. "First dibs on the shower." Melanie didn't protest, didn't move a muscle until she heard the glass door slide shut.

Melanie remembered some of that night. Camille propping her up and telling her she'd feel better if she puked, repeating that she needed to "get it all out, get it all out." Telling her that she should learn to control her drinking, that she'd embarrassed Camille and ruined her fun. That she was, in fact, a shitty friend. *Get it all out.*

The shame was almost worse than the throb in her head and the tight nausea that dissolved so slowly throughout the next day. She stayed cramped and curled in a dorm bed while Camille attended sessions on financial aid and choosing a major, collecting brochures for her. She'd resolved to be the best friend Camille ever had. And to never drink alcohol again, though that promise had only lasted until high school graduation.

Blinded by tears, Melanie jogged along the beach. She didn't care that it was private. What's the worst a wealthy beachfront property owner could do? Humiliate her? Been there. Hypnotize her to vote Republican? Already on her list of past crimes.

She ran until her lungs burned. She collapsed in damp sand the color of a storm. The sky was mottled with streaky clouds, shot through with gulls and cormorants. She wanted to call Tim, but she'd left her phone on the deck. She couldn't imagine what she'd say anyway. *You think sending a strange man to my door at night is messed up? Wait 'til you hear this one.*

The beach smelled like death. Rotting sea creatures secreted in shells that the gulls had missed. Bull kelp strewn along the sand like abandoned whips. This is what she'd come for? Her hair curled in puddled salt water, and she wondered how she'd ever get all the grains of broken rock and shell and fish poop out of her scalp. Maybe she should give up and let the ocean claim her.

Melanie propped on her elbows to watch a boat skimming the waves. The sun was high enough in the sky that the day had lost its crisp quality, the way morning light outlined everything. She started a slow walk back, reluctant to return. She studied the prints her feet left and scanned the sand for shells to bring back to the girls. She tried not to think about what Camille had said. What she'd implied. After several minutes of her trance-like walk, she saw a sand dollar half-buried, its mounded middle peeking out. She plucked it, saw it was unbroken, and rinsed the sand away in the waves so the shadowy petals stood out. She couldn't remember why they were called sand dollars. Maybe because you had to treasure and save them for a rainy day. She tucked it in her sweatshirt pocket.

"Jesus, Mel, you look like something snagged on the end of a hook." Camille was sipping coffee, her hair and makeup fresh, large sunglasses hiding her hangover.

"Don't fucking talk to me."

"Oh, for God's sake, honey, don't ruin the day. I've got it all planned out. We'll start at Ebey Bay, looking for those elusive baby seals, and we'll lunch in Coupeville. Then, drumroll please—I've got a surprise for you."

"I don't want any more of your surprises." Melanie opened the sliding glass door and went into the kitchen. Camille followed.

"You'll want this one. I've scheduled a massage for you! Billy told me about this guy whose hands just meld to your body."

"Fuck you. And Billy. Fuck him."

Camille sighed a long, dramatic exhale. Then, in a little girl's voice, "I don't understand this at all." She perched on one of the pine barstools at the kitchen counter. "We were having such a good time."

Melanie tried to look into her eyes to confirm that she really believed what she'd just said. But Camille was still wearing the oversized sunglasses so all Melanie saw was the distorted reflection of herself, the matted tendrils of her Medusa curls.

Next would come the pouting and the histrionics and the placating and pledging to be a better friend. And then it would be as if the tide came and washed away every last trace of it. Until the next time.

"Take the appointment yourself. Get the knots worked out." She wanted to speak with kindness, the way she spoke to her children when they'd crossed a

line only because they were tired or hungry, but her
words shot out like darts. "I've got other plans."

The rental car was leased in her name, and she knew it
would be a mistake to leave it behind, but she couldn't
abandon Camille to her own two feet. Melanie walked
her rolling suitcase to the island shuttle stop and
boarded a bus bound for Sea-Tac International. It felt
good to leave on the power of her own legs. She only
missed the car when the bus drove onto the ferry, onto
the middle bottom deck where, walled by steel, she
couldn't see the water splitting and rolling, the shore
receding and appearing again.

She closed her eyes and leaned on the cool window,
trying to decide whether the motion felt like bus or
boat, whether she was moving forward or floating or
both. When she woke, she was at the airport, the Seattle
skyline already behind her.

At the ticket counter, Melanie waited in line behind
two men in dress blues, and it struck her suddenly that
Marty Barker had gone straight into the navy after high
school. He wouldn't have been at a college party. Unless
he was on leave.

Her heart beat faster. He wouldn't have been on
leave. He would have been in a submarine, submerged
and contained in the deep. She was sure. *Yes*, she
thought. *I can be sure of that. Can't I?*

The airplane reached full speed at over 300 miles
an hour, but she felt deliciously still. The man in the
aisle seat didn't even glance her way, and she studied
the clouds and imagined Tim's delight when he returned
from the lab to find her home. She thought of the girls,
how after dinner, she would present the sand dollar like
proof of a perfect trip.

HARM'S WAY

Her hearing has never been any good, something her
mother blames on those teen years spent trapped
between the headphones of a portable stereo. Add to that
her love of kitsch in the form of a Gremlin, old rusting
car with a Swiss cheese muffler, and it's no surprise
she doesn't hear the water pump go as she's cruising
down I-29, singing with Tom Jones that Labor Day
weekend. It's not unusual—no, it's not unusual—until
Bette glances down at the gauges and sees the needle in
red, feels the nauseous swirl of adrenaline in her urgent
deceleration and prayerful glide to a complete stop on
the side of a busy highway an hour before dusk.

Steam snarling from the radiator, Bette pops the
hood, then jumps back, suddenly mindful of burns.
Shit, shit, shit. This mantra usually calms her, but it's
been two months since she's seen her boyfriend, and
she just sunk half a grand into this car for a corroded
steering column and a brake job, and she's afraid of

losing her job to computer graphics technology, and she can't help it—she cries. Big, gulping sobs that don't help her nausea any and only offend her pride.

Cars whizz past, farting exhaust in her face, grinding their mechanical gears into even her half-deaf ears. She wonders if she should wave somebody down, play the part of the helpless female. Bette's wearing the dress. A green chiffon number that Bill calls her "flirty skirt," which is why she wore it, so when they meet up at the Motel 6 in Branson, he'll want her all the more. Now with the wind of passing cars, she feels vulnerable the way the hem flutters up, teasing her with exposure. She *is* the helpless female, she realizes as she stares at the smoking front of her Gremlin.

Then, like a prayer answered, a semi truck slows, slides into the emergency lane ahead, and backs toward her, grunting all the while, and when the brakes squeal, she thinks of a pig and that line in *Deliverance* that Bill likes to quote: "Squeal like a pig." He says this just before grabbing her around the waist, just before she slaps his hands and laughs that he *is* a pig, just before she opens herself to him again and again. Bette touches her chest lightly with one hand, twinge of a wish for him by her side. With the other, she holds down that skirt and waits for the truck driver to come tell her it will all be okay. *Just let it set a minute and it'll start just fine. I promise.*

He is a squat man, hairy, with a friendly smile, not quite old enough to be her father. She doesn't recognize him, but his first words are "I remembered you."

"Excuse me?"

"I remembered you when I topped that hill and saw you sitting here. You passed me back in Nebraska. Couldn't hardly believe that crazy car could go so fast. Guess it couldn't."

Without hesitation, the man raises the hood all the way and begins to poke at hoses. "Damn hot," he says as he runs his fingertips over the radiator. Bette can feel the searing heat from a foot behind him and is shocked that he doesn't flinch. He peers close as his face can get, tugs a few parts, then waggles one stubby hand at her. She sees the grease-grooved lines, the calluses that keep him from feeling the pain.

"Water pump," he pronounces, slamming his hand emphatically on the side of the car with a ringing bang.

"Oh?" Bette tries to sound knowledgeable, but the syllable is flat and empty as the brown countryside. Only the road is alive with manic movement toward the long weekend escape, and not a one of those maniacs has stopped to help. Few bother to drift into the left lane, and Bette fears for the truck driver when he walks around the driver's side, a sports car yellow as a child's crayon sun zipping just two feet from him. He beckons for her to follow, and because she needs this Good Samaritan too much to question, she braves the short walk, wincing when a minivan speeds past.

He points to her rear window, where a fine mist lacquers the glass. "See. That's from your water pump."

Dumbly, "But I thought it was in the front of the car." A semitrailer roars past and her skirt turns up like a smile on the warm wave of air.

The man nods. "But when she goes, water sprays down. On the highway it'll just sweep under the car and spray up the back window. Soon as you saw the water you should have stopped immediately." Bette hangs her head some, thinks about protesting that she'd driven through a puddle or something, but it's been bone dry this summer and they both know she just wasn't paying attention. It's a tendency of hers. At the medical lab where she works, she didn't pay attention to all those emails and flyers for computer workshops, and now she's the only one of twelve graphic artists who sends her drawings out of lab to get them camera-ready for the medical textbooks and charts.

Bette has been told by employers and clients that she's talented, but her only talent of late is the art of

increasing her own dispensability. That bill from D&D
Printing for finishing her circulatory system gave
Heather, her supervisor, a fit. "I'm warning you, Bette,"
she said, deliberately pronouncing the silent *e.* "You've
got to get with the program. I should charge this bill
against your next paycheck." When Heather finally
sashayed from the room, Bette mumbled, "Charge this,"
raising her middle finger like a flagless pole.

Her favorite co-workers had giggled until Heather
swerved back to ask what was funny, and they buried
their noses in software manuals while Bette pretended
to adjust her glasses with the offending finger.

"Is it going to be easy to fix?" Remembering the
credit card she promised she'd cut up but didn't, she
sighs measured relief, still shaking from adrenaline.
"Mr. Ummmm . . . ?"

He doesn't take the hint, and she decides they're not
in a cordial social situation anyway. Secretly she takes to
thinking of him by function, "Truck Driver," and that's
what she calls him in her head. Truck Driver taps a can
of chewing tobacco on the roof of her Gremlin, stuffs
his lip full, and nods. Mangles the words "Lucky that
fan stopped short of going right through the radiator.
Then you'd have troubles."

Like she doesn't have troubles now—car stuck
somewhere between Omaha and Kansas City, boyfriend
traveling to meet her in Branson where she won't be, the
evening light becoming more ominous the longer she
jaws with a Samaritan who has yet to prove his goodness.

"So what should I do? Can you call for a tow?" Bette
struggles to keep the whine out of her voice. She is thirty,
feels half that.

He leans now against the back of his truck as
if to think, and Bette notices for the first time the
inconspicuous bumper sticker: Jesus Saves. In a lighter
moment, say if he were just changing her tire at a truck
stop with phones and food and bathrooms, she might
ask if he were Jesus. They'd share a laugh and she'd

bum a smoke before tipping him her last ten-dollar bill for his efforts. But she's shivering and sweating and panicky with fear of being abandoned. She asks again if he'll call someone.

"Can't call a tow." He shakes his head almost sadly. "All I've got is a CB radio. But I can try to reach another southbound to call from the truck station up the way. Only about twenty miles from here in St. Joe."

"Couldn't you go call? If you're not too busy, I mean. I know it's a holiday and all."

"Oh, the family can wait. I've only got to get to K.C. and then we're off to Branson."

Bette perks up. "That's where I'm going." She wants to ask him where to go when she gets there, which campy show. Two things stop her. The first is that he appears to be someone who takes the Entertainment Capital of the Midwest very seriously. The second is what he says next.

"Besides, I couldn't leave you alone on the highway after what happened to that little girl, Gina Spong." A long stream of tobacco shoots from his mouth onto the roadside, splats on a hamburger wrapper like he'd meant to aim there. Bette wipes perspiration from her brow, then folds her arms at her sides, looking mostly at her still-steaming car.

"Spong? What kind of name is that?" She's cross now, something of a lesson in what he's saying, and she feels rebellious against it.

He looks at her sternly. "She disappeared last February on this stretch of road. Her car broke down." He raises an eyebrow to punctuate his point. "I've got a daughter about your age," he adds, as if he must explain his chivalry.

"I'm older than I look," Bette shoots back. "But maybe you should try to reach someone? Before it gets dark?"

The truck driver looks to the west, all golden and slipping dark. He jumps to his feet, clopping off to the cab in boots that echo on the pavement so loudly it's as if the traffic has been muted. Bette shivers again, despite the warm August evening. She thinks of the only two things she can. Bill driving his new, reliable Nissan toward Branson, expecting her to be there warming the bed. They've been apart seven months since he took a new finance job five hours away from her. He says he needs the benefits, the insurance, which Bette understands, and the retirement plan, which she doesn't.

And she thinks of Gina, whoever she is, however old, however frightened, just whisked off the road. Disappeared. She's never heard of this case, this name. She's not from Missouri. But she's seen enough movies to understand the threat of the open road. Bette has no reason not to believe Truck Driver, but the longer he's out of her sight, the more frantic her heartbeat. By the time he's back she has convinced herself that he is the one who took Gina, her body rotting in the back of his Jesus Saves rig.

Clop, clop. "Smart asses," he mutters. "I couldn't get anything but people with the wrong ideas about what to do with you." He spits and fixes his face into a disapproving scowl. "Guess you'd better ride into town with me. We'll call from there."

Bette stares out at the highway, where cars, their headlights just aglow, race past. She wonders why not one of them stops. She's in the Midwest where people are supposed to be friendly and helpful. Not that she's ever expected that in Omaha. Cities are different. And maybe because this is the road between Omaha and Kansas City, two of the largest cities in the area, she's lucky even this driver stopped. Maybe.

Seeing her hesitation, Truck Driver kindly suggests, "We can wait a while longer. Maybe someone really did stop and call."

"Thank you."

They stand in the emergency lane for nearly fifteen minutes, listening to cars and, in the traffic gaps, the crickets that sing from hidden clumps of grass. She looks for a mile marker, sees only an ordinary post, a red-winged blackbird bobbling there. She looks at her watch and thinks how she would be all the way through Kansas City by now with just three hours left on her trip. She would have switched to the B-52's tape, flicked on her headlights, too, searching out stretches where she could flood the road with her brights.

"So what's your name anyway?" he asks her in a short, traffic-free space.

Why? So you can give the next stranded girl a good detail? She hates herself for thinking this way. He didn't have to stop. "Bette."

"As in, lucky?"

"Jury's still out on that."

"I'm Bill," he answers.

"Ha! Am I on *Candid Camera* or something?" She plays nervously with her hemline. *Always wanted to die in Bill's arms. That God and His wacky sense of humor.* She looks at Bill the Truck Driver's perplexed expression and explains, "My boyfriend's name too."

"Oh," he says. "I see." And he says it so it's obvious that he has no idea what she's babbling about, which is something Bette hates.

A car's tires squeal a sudden swerve away from the Gremlin, obscured now in the waning light, and Bill the Truck Driver grunts. "I've got to go. Mary Jane will wonder where I am. She might be getting worried by now." He looks tired, his face drawn down by evening shadows. Or is it malice the shadows unmask?

"I can't drive even to the next town?" A little girl's voice now, collapsed in the wind.

"Not even a mile. You'll ruin the radiator, probably crack the engine block. I can call you some help in St. Joe, but the offer for a ride is still good." He jangles his keys, hint of impatience as she stands frozen to the concrete between her dead Gremlin and the massive truck.

Bette sighs. "I just need to grab my bag."

In the car, out of Bill the Truck Driver's sight, she clutches her keys in the ignition, then sees with alarm that her pepper spray canister is no longer attached. That flight to Chicago last weekend for a friend's wedding. A weapon, the airline had said, and she'd had to keep it at the ticket counter where it still waits in a shoebox for the lost and found. Frantically, she roots around in her leather satchel for another possible weapon. Her sketch pad, a tube of lip balm, wallet, loose receipts, two pencils—one dull, one broken. She fumbles through it again: loose receipts, sketch pad, broken pencil, lip balm, dull pencil, wallet. She decides on the dull pencil, keeps it hidden in her right hand. The bag goes over her shoulder, and the door is locked and slammed before she remembers her keys still swinging in the ignition. She turns to Bill, but he is gone, waiting in the cab. Her heart clenches and she mutters, "Bette, be calm."

With measured, exacted, falsified calm, she slowly rips a piece of paper from her sketchbook and prints with the dull pencil a note: *I, Bette Rankin, am in this truck. Please call police in case I'm not back.* She draws an arrow to a corner of the page where she sketches in fine but quick detail the back of the truck, complete with license plate and truck number. She starts the bumper sticker but only gets through "Jesus" when the truck's loud, strange horn alarms her. Quickly, she jots the time, folds the paper and places it carefully under a windshield wiper. With one glance back, she walks toward the cab.

Higher than she expected to ride, the seat bouncier. It might be fun if it weren't for the country music station and all that business with the car and that other girl. Gina.

"So this girl that disappeared on the highway. I never heard about her." Right hand tightens on the pencil.

"That was a lot of months back." He pauses for a long time, waiting for another truck to pass so he can wave.

"Do you know him?"

"Nope. We wave at all the drivers. It's important to have allies on the road." He turns down the twang and continues. "College girl driving home from somewhere that January or February. Car broke down, and app-arently someone stopped to help. Bastard kidnapped her. That's the cops' best guess anyway. The car was still there on the roadside next day. No sign of Gina Spong."

Bette watches the mile markers, knows they've still got a good fifteen minutes in the cab. "Spong is a weird name though, isn't it?" It's the best she can do, weary and wary, but she wishes the words away when she sees him scowl. "I just haven't heard it before."

"Everyone's heard it around here now," he says. "Gonna keep hearing it until they find the body or the killer or both." Then he switches conversational gears and Bette drops her pencil. "So what are you going to do in Branson?"

"Do a little dance, make a little love." The song lyrics blurt from her mouth, a nervous, wise-ass response that would be entirely appropriate with those co-workers who still think the finger is funny. Not with a stranger who she suspects might murder her. She finishes weakly, "Get down tonight?"

Bill the Truck Driver looks at her like she's crazy. It's a look she's seen on Bill the Boyfriend's face too many times. "It's a tape I have in my car." More explanation. *It's my boyfriend's name too. I've been too busy for those computer workshops. The dog ate my homework. She reminded me of you.* Explanation. As if it ever helps.

The truck driver launches into a description of some band in Branson. The Backwood Boys or Breakneck Brothers or something like that. Bette spends the next ten miles flinching every time his hands move toward her to adjust the radio or shift gears. The rest of the time she thinks of better responses to that question: "So what are you going to do when you get to Branson?"

She settles for the uninspired and inoffensive, "I'm going to enjoy everything the Entertainment Capital of the Midwest has to offer," because she doesn't yet know what that is. She's prepared then when Bill the Truck Driver actually exits in St. Joseph and leaves her—

unmolested—at a truck stop where she is eventually
asked that same question. And, oddly, most people
ask this sometime after bringing up the ghost of Gina
Spong. It takes on an ominous tone juxtaposed that
way, and they all ask: the woman at the service station,
the tow truck driver who cracks the window to get her
keys, the clerk at the Motel 6 in St. Joseph, Missouri,
where she's forced to spend the night. She gives them
the standard answer, and they each smile in turn like
she's a pet performing a trick.

Bette tries to explain why the question bothers her
so much when Bill, her Bill, returns her message to the
motel in Branson where they were supposed to meet. She
tries to tell him how the service station woman looked
when she first thought Bette had hitchhiked. *Don't you
remember what happened to Gina Spong?* She wants
him to see her through the young motel clerk's eyes:
a girl with a flimsy dress, a bag, and a small suitcase,
leaping from a stranger's tow truck.

Instead she cries into the phone until he agrees to
drive up to stay while her Gremlin is fixed. He says
he'll keep their reservations for the next two nights.
Irritation in his tone or just static in the line?

She turns on the television, straight to free HBO, and
lets the action movie blast gunfire into the room while
she imagines Bill's routine. He'll apologize twice to the
motel people, and he'll gas up the car and rearrange
his CD's, and then he'll buy a packet of caffeine pills
because he won't want to stop to pee. She expects him
no later than 2:30 in the morning.

A movie and two PBS specials on air disasters later,
Bette can't stay awake. She tries to practice early sketches
for her next project: the inner ear, a chart for elementary
school students to study before they go in to have their
hearing checked. Everything an educational experience
these days. She finds a scratchy blue ballpoint in the
same drawer with the Holy Bible (which says nothing
about the Gideons—she checks). Detailed work always

perks her energy. Though she hardly seems the type for detail anywhere else in her life, Bette excels on this point at work, and as she begins to outline the coil of the ear and the canal, she brightens, remembering how good she is, *talented*, even with ordinary ink. They can't let her go. She's only begun to shade the anvil bone when she slumps to sleep atop the bedspread.

She wakes in another adrenaline jack-up, terror split seconds before the realization that the pounding must be Bill, that he is late, that she's fallen asleep and creased a line in her drawing, inner and outer ear permanently separated by one simple, careless fold.

A cautious peek from behind heavy beige curtains and she sees her boyfriend soaked from late-night rain, trying to keep himself dry under his duffel bag. Instantly she swings the locks and frees the chain to open the door and gather him into her arms, recoiling some from the cold, the wet, the sweat she smells on him. As he locks back up and flings aside his duffel for a better hug, Bette begins to sob again.

"Hey," he whispers, patting her back quickly and without rhythm, "I'm here now."

"You're late," she moans, though until just that moment it hadn't bothered her.

Bill guides her to one of the double beds. They both sit, and he flops back, exhaustion a blanket on his face, smothering his features, eroding the sharper angles. If Bette sketched him now, she would want that dull pencil lost in another Bill's truck cab.

"There was an accident a few hours back, and we were at a full stop for over twenty minutes. It was horrible, Bette. Something was covered with a sheet, and I know it wasn't a deer."

She blanches at the thought and squeezes his arm. "I'm so glad you're okay."

"Me too," he sighs. "I've driven a lot more than I'd planned to tonight. I felt myself fading a couple of times." Bill hugs her close, kisses her forehead, which leads to her cheek, to her lips, to her neck, back up to her lips, and she can almost hear the song in her head: "The knee bone's connected to the shin bone. . . . The cheekbone's connected to the neck bone."

Their lovemaking—the first in months—is short and sweet.

Bill is asleep in minutes, gentle snore starting up like a purr. Bette snuggles into him, almost asleep until she thinks of Gina Spong. Who did she make love to last? Or is she still alive, still making love in some desperate human wedge against mortality? Maybe she feigned her own disappearance to escape with an old flame. These fantasies tease Bette for several minutes as she thinks of Gina living somewhere exotic and out of harm's way. She's in Tahiti wearing a peasant's blouse, slurping daiquiris on the beach, laughing when she sees a story on CNN Satellite News that mentions a plain old state like Missouri, glad to have escaped.

Gina in Denver or Minneapolis working at an ice cream shop in the airport, where she dreams every day about which flight she'll sneak onto, which city she'll explore next. Gina Spong who is now Jennifer or Amy, something that will blend in with her generation, a woman who convinced her boyfriend to disappear and change his name to Matt or Rob.

She kisses Bill's arm to watch it react, and it jerks away like something separate and untamed. She realizes that he forgot to ask about the car and the road and all the danger she's felt coldly present as a ghost at her back all night.

By morning, Bill has perked up, enthused again about the road and Branson. He has a brochure in one hand that reads: *JESSICA!* A pretty, overly made-up blond grins on the cover. Barbie with a Southern bouffant and a shiny red satin shirt that matches her lipstick. Her show is touted as one of the most popular in town, and Bill grins when he reads an excerpt about how Jessica sings a unique blend of country, gospel, and jazz. "You'd have to hear it to believe it," he quotes, tugging on Bette's sleeve as she clings to the pillow that blocks her eyes from sunlight.

"What about the car?" she mumbles. "And coffee. I need coffee."

"I have Vivarin. And we'll swing by in an hour for the car. They know what to do, right?"

Bette rolls slowly to face the day, sure it will be better than the last. "The tow truck driver knows the mechanic. He was supposed to call or leave a note, but we better check. And you know I don't do my caffeine in any form but java."

After quick showers and a stop at a gas station that sells "gourmet" coffee, which turns out to be nothing more than flavored Folgers, they arrive at the garage and Bette sighs to see the Gremlin parked in the exact same spot where it was left the night before. Turns out the driver hasn't called anyone yet, so Bette explains about the water pump, and the eager young mechanic says sure he can get to it today but probably not until afternoon. "Plenty of water pumps in stock," he says.

"Bill? What do you want to do? Not until afternoon."

"Drive to Branson. We've got reservations."

"And the car? How will I get back here?"

"I'll drive you, Bette. We'll just have to leave earlier than planned, huh?" He rubs her arm gently. She can see in his eyes that he's tired of waiting.

"Okay."

Bette signs all the necessary forms at the mechanic's desk and smiles appreciatively when the young man tells her to have a great weekend in Branson. He doesn't ask what she'll do, never once mentions the name Gina Spong, and it's like a curse has been lifted this cloudless morning.

The drive is a pleasant one, reminding Bette of the early days of this relationship, when they were students, an art major and a business major driving the Iowa back roads, dreaming of where they'd start an art colony. Bill, who loved all the senior show paintings she said were inspired by him (only a white lie, she's assured herself many times over), was sure he could make such a plan profitable. They'd talked about a farmhouse south of Dubuque or somewhere near the Amana colonies. They haven't talked about their dream in years.

"We could start our art colony in St. Joe," she teases as they roll smoothly along the crowded highway.

He looks confused, then smiles and pats her leg. "Oh that. You don't paint anymore."

"I paint sometimes in my head," Bette answers. "I imagine what scenes would look like in bright Fauve colors. Like us driving down this highway right now. We'd have golds and greens blocked on the canvas at an angle to suggest changing seasons and motion."

"Green and gold. The colors of money," he teases.

"You're a stereotype."

"I'll be a rich one." He mimes smoking a cigar and turns up the stereo a notch.

Bette feels her sadness sink and thicken like paint left uncapped. She's not sad that he's an avid capitalist but that she isn't. She thinks of her rusted and broken Gremlin as they glide over the pavement in his well-tuned sedan. His computer expertise, manipulating any machine like a servant or a lover. Her fear of everything digital, loving instead the archaic scratch of pencil on paper and the physicality of erasing. No "Delete" button to do her dirty work for her.

She wonders now why he would even marry her, if indeed he plans to. She's never brought it up, not even as an "if we ever got married." He's always so disparaging about their married friends. But other people have started asking, especially since Bill moved to St. Louis: her mother, her college friends, even her shy father, who said, "Well, um, when do you think he might make an honest woman of you?"

Before the siren's call of self-pity can begin, Bette pulls herself away and toward some hot country song on the radio that she doesn't mind singing along to.

"Getting psyched up for Jessica?" Bill teases. She nods, covers his hand where it rests needlessly on the automatic gear shift.

Jessica is all the brochure promised and more. Glitzy, sunny, flirty, croony. The crowd laps her up, and Bette is pleased. This is what she came for. Jessica sings "Thank God I'm a Country Girl" backed up by guys in chaps who actually start a kick line and eventually carry Jessica off stage and back in for her encore.

"To think I could have been stuck in St. Joseph," she whispers, her mouth close to Bill's ear. He leans in, mouth smelling of yeasty beer.

"What is Joseph the saint of anyway?" he murmurs.

"I'm not Catholic."

"Play along."

Bette's creativity shrivels in the face of demands for it. She shrugs. "Let's just get back to the hotel room before everyone else rushes out of here."

Bill glances around the crowded room at the clientele, most of them wearing T-shirts a size too small and drunken grins a size too large. He nods and ushers her out the door, past the autographed photos of Jessica that Bette almost wants for a souvenir. "God Bless and Keep You! Love, Jessica." A large, sloppy circle over the "i."

"It's as good as a St. Christopher medallion," Bette tries to argue for a photograph as she's pushed toward the car.

"What's Christopher the saint of?"

"Travel. I know that one."

"Not well enough, obviously."

Their two-mile drive to the motel takes forty minutes in a bumper-to-bumper crawl. This town was never meant to handle such traffic, especially on a Saturday night of Labor Day weekend. Bill curses every few feet, paranoid that someone will accelerate too fast and hit the car. Bette curses silently, wanting to be back in the room, wanting urgently to make love because she knows she's being sent back the next day. That's how it feels. Like being sent back home from a wonderful place as some sort of punishment for a misdemeanor she's never been publicly accused of.

In the room, she takes extra time in the bathroom, primping, something she almost never does. She toys with the short curls around her face, adjusts the straps of a nightie she picked up at the Goodwill, though she won't tell Bill that part. She rubs scented lotion into her shoulders and finally flounces out to greet him, hoping to make up for the fact that he never saw her in her flirty skirt yesterday.

Bill is propped on a pillow watching CNN. "Damn," he says. "Princess Diana was in an accident. Her boyfriend was killed."

"Breaking News" appears at the bottom of the screen, and for a confused moment, before the idiom makes sense, Bette wonders how news can break. Does it fall apart like an old car or snap into jagged halves like some cartoon heart?

"Jesus." She realizes that she had no idea the princess even had a boyfriend, and she would never admit in public that she'd been one of thousands of American girls to set her alarm very early to watch the wedding. "Is she okay?"

"Broke her arm," Bill says, and with her faulty hearing Bette thinks at first that he's said *Broken charm.* "Maybe internal injuries. They're not sure yet. You can't be too careful." He scrunches his face like he's thinking about their drive back to St. Joseph the next day. Bette starts thinking about her drive down, the Gremlin suddenly going hot, her panic at being alone. She wonders if the princess even knows what's happened to her lover, and Bette feels her heart swell with the sadness of all that loss. Husband to divorce, lover to car crash. Then she can't help but think of Gina Spong, some natural progression to that ghost of a girl who disappeared on the road, for better or for worse nobody knows. Though somebody somewhere does know, and that's what bothers Bette most.

"This is too horrible," Bette snaps. "Turn it off."

"Don't you even want to find out?"

"No!"

Bill looks surprised at her tone, pauses as if to say more, reconsiders, and turns off the television. He draws her into his arms again. She sniffles but can't generate tears.

"I'm being silly, aren't I?"

No response, just a tighter hug.

"I just don't want you to leave me, that's all. I hate the distance. I hate the open road." She suspects right away that she means something metaphorical in that last part, but she doesn't stop to think about it. "I hate not knowing if we'll make it."

Bill pulls away to look at her, and she wonders briefly if that gloss in his eyes is sincerity or anxiety. "We'll make it," he finally insists, then repeats to seal the deal, sign on the dotted line, promise her the wide, wide world complete with money-back guarantee. "We'll make it."

They make gentle love that night, the soft sea-rhythm that leaves Bette teary-eyed and deeper in love after these eight, almost nine, years. She sleeps solidly in his arms, forgetting that no mechanics work on Sundays or Labor Days, still unaware that it is more than a water pump, more than a broken arm. Unaware because nobody, she'll later decide, ever wants to stop the forward motion, the sweet giddy joy of speeding on and on in the same senseless direction. It takes something bigger, something or someone outside yourself, to change that. Laws of physics that everyone has to obey—beautiful princesses; college girls forever on their way home; graphic artists floating along behind the times, hoping to ride in the draft; and the Other Woman in St. Louis, who will enjoy her whirling single life until Bill stops her cold with a diamond that Bette will always imagine as big as a water pump.

TERESA OF PIERCE COUNTY, NEBRASKA

Some nights on the prairie when a thunderstorm seizes the house in its teeth and shakes, I go outside. Pelted to a sopping mess in seconds, I lie down in the open yard. I finger the tiny silver cross at my throat, and I pray for God to strike. I'm not a saint. I'm an atheist, a woman for whom God deflated like a helium balloon. Tied to the post of my double bed, He sunk day by day until finally I threw the wrinkled skin away.

But a storm will splash light into dark corners and show you how empty and dusty they've become. It will make you shudder and wish for something to rise again.

If that something is airy, insubstantial, the very thing that could rise, like a ghost, I can't cling. Faith is my problem. Where is the tentacle of the unseen with which I can hook a hand around the impossible?

And so I want to be struck.

Don't get me wrong—I'm not one of those women who'd take a mortal man's fist for love. My husband

never raised his hands against me; they were buried in
soil all his life and now in death. But God. If God is
going to love you, it better be more than a whispered
sweet nothing, more than the easy escape of air.

I lie there those rare, spectacular nights, and as I
sputter for breath, blind and cold, my lids light up pink,
and I imagine that blazing spear piercing my heart. The
electric motion of creation searing through my blood
and singing my nerves. I know I'd be a monster ever
after. But some moments are worth their ever after.

This is not about my husband. I miss him less than I
miss God, though I believed in him more. But one night
in July when the air smelled burnt and the storm was
more bark than bite, I lay motionless, eyes wide. I saw
the white-hot cracks sawing the clouds, the branches of
my weeping willow sweeping restlessly. And I thought
how if I were as tall as a tree, I could bring down one of
those bolts. Then I could see and feel God again.

I rose slowly to my feet. A long flash suspended the
sky and my breath, and that's when I saw them: a pair
of pheasants huddled in a thicket of raspberry bushes I
never harvested anymore. I rushed them, flushed them
out like the storm couldn't. Panicked flaps against the
wind, soft bodies battered by forces that never mean
harm. I hooked my heart to the smallest one and sent it
like a love note to any god with true aim.

SCORCHER, 1979

Someday it won't burn, this smoke searing her lungs. And that, thinks Sylvie, after a long cigarette drag that shortens her breath, is when everything else will.

No rain on the high plains for over a month. Grass parched, high nineties. Everyone wants to be somewhere else, even the birds hiding in the shade trees, but the oil crisis lingers. The travel agency is like a funeral home but with better lighting and bright posters of toothy flight attendants who look down on her all day. She walks outside on her smoke breaks, even in the heat.

Linda is still there, smoking by the door, so she can rush for the phone. Sylvie slows and pulls fiercely on the too-short cigarette. Burns the backs of her fingers. Yelps and drops it to smolder on the sidewalk.

"Stamp that out," Linda warns, rubbing hers into the brick wall where she leans. Another charred hatch marking time.

"Yes," chirps Sylvie. "Fire safety!"

First, Smokey the Bear, then her smokejumper boyfriend, now a woman who thinks she's everybody's mother. Sylvie stomps on the butt, grinding it with her shoe until the heel snaps.

"Damn! Why do these things happen to me?"

Linda shakes her head.

"Is that the phone?" Sylvie asks. She watches her co-worker scurry inside. Alone, she breathes the warm, clean air, hand pressed to her aching chest.

"Pranksters," Linda says when Sylvie limps inside and sits at her desk beneath a beautiful brunette encouraging her to fly the friendly skies.

The phone rings for real then, her line. "Hi, baby," the smokejumper says. She leans back in her chair, props her broken shoe on the desk.

"Dropped your cigarettes," Linda calls, tossing them in Sylvie's lap.

"Cigarettes?" the smokejumper echoes like he's never heard of them. "Since when do you smoke?"

"Since you left for the third time this month," Sylvie says, remembering the way last night's cowboy let his cigarette dangle from under his moustache. The scorched, tickling kiss.

"I don't create the fires. I just fight them."

"And how's this one?"

"Hot and dangerous. Like you."

"But you don't create fires. You just fight them, remember? And I don't go anywhere, just help everyone else live their escape fantasies."

He clears his throat. "Baby, I'm calling to apologize. For the other night. I shouldn't have called you that." She invokes her right to remain silent. "You're not a whore." She twirls the broken shoe. "Please. Say something."

"Stay safe," she says, her throat unexpectedly hoarse. "I gotta go." A young couple walks in. Linda's gone to the back for typewriter ribbon.

"Welcome," Sylvie says, baring her teeth in a smile. She needs this commission.

"It's a scorcher out there," the man says, mopping his neck with his own shirt collar while his wife fumbles for a handkerchief.

"Alaska?" Sylvie points to the colorful brochures on her desk. The man fans himself with Las Vegas.

"Somewhere cool, but not that cool," chimes the wife. "Maybe the mountains."

"Vegas is great if you're feeling lucky," Sylvie drawls, holding the man's gaze until he drops his eyes.

"Cooler," his wife repeats.

"Jamaica? Aruba? You can go anywhere. Depends what you're willing to pay." Each syllable sparks on her lips, trying to catch.

CONTROLLED BURN

On those prairie nights, parked in a cornfield, she could reduce herself to a single point on the vast grid of back roads and rail crossings. Mapping the self. The radiant stars above were her mirror map. If she could locate herself on the coordinates of a flat Nebraska landscape, she could look up anywhere, anytime, and find herself reflected, an observable point in all of vast space. She could say it with certainty—*still here*.

In the cobalt night, with Fen behind her, gripping her hips so hard she bit her lip and tasted blood, Marly recognized from the vault of memory this end-of-season smell—dry dirt, withered vegetation. That long ago October morning they had found her baby brother blue in his crib and her mother had howled—a sound more terrifying than what escaped the closed door on nights her parents drank the whole bottle of wine with dinner and hustled her to bed too early. That morning she'd slipped into the yard, alone in her nightgown, the air had smelled the same, like an ending. That day she had seen leaving their house: a toy box (full), her father, a small bundle of blankets, the pastor from the church they went to on Easter and Christmas, and a quart of milk her mother had flung out the back door as if it had gone bad when Marly knew it hadn't because they'd given some to the baby before bedtime. She'd had a glass too.

Marly reached back, wrapped a hand over Fen's and said, "Stop."

"Too late," he panted. "Oh. Omigod." Spasm into collapse, his weight on her back almost knocking them both to their knees. "Sorry."

Headlights, wavering and bumping in the distance, flashed like meteors.

She pulled away, letting everything spill to the dirt below. She imagined children, their eyes sealed tight as buds, their baby teeth small, square, and even as corn nibs, sprouting up in that same spot.

She fumbled into her panties, smoothed down her skirt, and wriggled her feet into slip-on sandals. She hugged her own arms, running her fingers over the prickle of goosebumps. Fen pulled up his jeans. He stretched and gently beat his chest like a gorilla. She laughed.

"I tried to stop," he mumbled, pulling her to him for a kiss that she resisted, her bitten lip pulsing. He buried his face in her neck instead. In the island of her mind, she thought how there was only ever try, how she wanted more do and done.

He rested his thumb on his lips, staring off in the distance. She'd seen this gesture before, like he'd started his life as a thumbsucker.

"You're going to start this truck, take me to my place, go home to your kids, and kiss them on the cheek while they sleep."

She felt his disappointment in the sudden sag of his body and the cool swirl of air where his mouth had been moments before, but she never regretted reminding him of the facts of his life.

"It's not a punishment," she said. But she felt like a punisher.

"Car," Fen warned. Marly knew the drill; she tucked her head, closed her eyes. Nebraska was one of the states with the least amount of light pollution, where the stars you wouldn't see anywhere else popped out of the black backdrop. Protect your night vision or all those stars disappeared, slow to return.

"You got your ID?" Fen asked as the car slowed and the headlights made a sharp swing from the road, trapping them in dual spotlights.

"Cop?"

He nodded, and she remembered the policeman who'd found her that October morning when she was eight and her baby brother was blue and still. She'd hidden, not well enough, in a thicket of trees beyond their backyard. He'd said that her parents were all torn up, that she didn't need to make it worse, and he insisted on holding her hand as they walked back, like she'd run away if he didn't. (She would have.)

"Nice night," the state trooper called out, a silhouette moving cautiously.

"I'm not here," she whispered to Fen. But he'd already stepped forward, hands up in the air.

"I swear I didn't touch her," he joked. What a dumbass he could be.

She stepped forward too. "We were looking at stars, trying to pick out constellations. Just enjoying one of the last decent evenings before winter sets in and we're stuck inside."

She smiled what she knew to be her most charming smile (it had worked on Fen and many men before him), but it was dark, and her moonlit teeth probably looked demonic, and she thought suddenly how she should break away, run blindly down the dark gravel road. Right now.

She chose the corn, or rather the corn stubble that scraped her ankles and then stabbed her foot when her first sandal went flying just a few fumbling steps into that halfhearted run, an embarrassment worse than Fen's gorilla arms in the air because nobody chased her. Fen and the trooper stood, shadows in the headlights, leafless trees, empty stalks. Patient. Maybe even a little bored, as though women ran away from them all the time.

"Ma'am—I'm talking to *her*, sir—is everything okay?" the trooper called. "Has he done anything?"

She could hear Fen swearing softly to himself, but she didn't turn around; she watched a satellite unspooling in the sky before her. Nothing was as fixed as it looked at first glance. Her mouth tasted salty like Fen's, which must have tasted like his wife's, which probably tasted like somebody else. She heard the trooper commanding her to turn around slowly and come back, and she spat at her feet, trying to get some new-old taste out of her mouth. Part blood, part salt, part something else.

Has he done anything? What had Fen ever done? Not much.

She turned, the ball of her foot stepping painfully on the edge of a rock so she cried out. She limped forward, returning to the truck while the trooper shifted nervously. She smelled smoke and glanced at Fen to see the cherry of a cigarette flaring as he inhaled. Like he was trying to light his mouth on fire.

"You're not under arrest," the trooper was telling him, "But you need to answer my questions."

"I won't kiss you when you've been smoking, you know." Fen flicked his eyes at her, annoyed. She imagined his children, a boy and girl, tucked in bed. They deserved an "I love you" and a kiss that didn't taste of cigarettes and the saliva of some woman who wasn't their mother.

She'd kissed her baby brother every night before he went in his crib, big sloppy kisses on his forehead that made him giggle. How poorly she'd slept after that crib was taken away. She'd watched that leave the house too. No more children, her mother always said, living her words like a commandment, dating only men who weren't interested in family, not even their own.

The trooper chided them both for parking on private property and lectured them on how to behave when being questioned by a man with a gun. "For god's sake," he said, voice dropping momentarily into a conversational tone. "I could have shot you. All this way out of town you might have been drug dealers."

Marly bit the inside of her lip to stop from laughing, then winced at the tenderness. *Drug dealers out here? Would you like some coke with all that popcorn?* Though in the Midwest it was more likely to be meth, something cheap and sad.

"I come out here for the stars," she said, realizing that was true. Fen was a distraction, always had been. A ride to this place where she felt she could breathe.

In the light of his car's headlights, the trooper looked from the hem of her short skirt all the way down her bare legs. Then his expression softened. "Your feet . . ."

They were a scratched and bloody mess, both of them. Fen was still smoking, but he turned away from her to exhale, stubbed the butt into the dirt at his feet and reached a hand out to caress the foot closest to him. She gasped at the bite of his touch on raw flesh.

"Don't leave that," the trooper warned, and so Fen cradled the butt in his palm like something newly hatched.

"Are we free to go?" Fen asked.

The trooper hesitated, glancing at Marly's feet. "Are you going to get her some medical care? Clean those cuts?"

"Of course."

"I really should run your plates first."

"Run 'em then." Fen pulled the cigarettes from his jacket pocket again, and Marly stared at the trooper, who was younger than he sounded, no creases around his eyes, the first place she'd noticed her own aging. Cornfield drug dealers? He'd just let a man he didn't know reach into a hidden pocket. He'd let a woman bolt twenty feet out of reach. He hadn't even run their plates first. They could be Bonnie and Clyde, Caril Ann Fugate and Charles Starkweather. But really, they were too old for that.

"Yes," Marly said. "Run his plates. You'll find out his name is Fenway Briggs, and he owns this truck along with his wife, Amanda, and their address is 125 Belle Air Court, and every Thursday night his two children watch him leave that address for a band practice that doesn't exist." Her eyes welled. "I don't think there's even a band."

"There's a band!" Fen stabbed at the air with an unlit cigarette.

"I'm going to run these plates now," the trooper said, backing away. When neither of them complained, he turned to the safety of his two-way radio and on-board computer.

"I have a band."

"So you've told me." Marly wiped at her eyes. "I wish that guy would hurry. It's cold out here."

"You've never heard me play guitar. Played it 'til my fingers bled."

"Fen, that's a song lyric. You didn't just make that up."

"I don't need this." He turned and stared into the black fields. He lit another cigarette, smoke snaking his head. When had he started smoking so much? She could see the nickel-sized beginnings of a bald spot. *At least women are spared that*, she thought.

When the trooper returned, he said, "You can go."

"That's it? You're not even going to give us a warning?"

"Marly!" Fen barked. "He's letting us go."

"You got your warning. Gotta report to an accident on 80. You two have a nice night. Somewhere else." He tipped his hat—quaintly old-fashioned—and started back to his car.

They stood in silence in the remains of the year's corn crop, and Marly listened to the man's soft footsteps in the dirt, the wind in her ear and the few, stubborn, end-of-season crickets sawing their songs, the gentle hoot of an owl cloaked in darkness. Fen threw his cigarette into the field, and she imagined a dry stalk catching, the whole field a symphony of flame and heat. Farmers sometimes burned their fields to restore fertility to the soil. Controlled burns. But the smoke could get so bad people couldn't see to drive. Contain one thing, and another escapes.

"I have a band," Fen insisted. "You should hear us play some time. Maybe when we get our first gig."

"Name?"

"What?"

"Of the band?"

"I'm taking suggestions."

She sighed and hobbled toward the truck, hoping he'd take that suggestion. But the police car was still parked and she waited for Fen to catch up, watching the trooper, who appeared to be bent over, reading something on the hood of his vehicle. Then he slid to the ground.

"Oh my god! Are you okay?" She ran to the man's side, her stupid sandals flying off again, her feet stinging.

His face looked too white, but the moonlight and the shadows of the headlights played tricks. It was his eyes that alarmed her, distant, unfocused, soft like they were seeing more than she knew was there. "Feel sick," he whispered. He closed his eyes, breath whistling from his nose.

Fen was already on it, cell phone in hand, face illuminated by the glow of the screen. "Reception's weak." Of course. That was partly why they drove out all this way, so he couldn't check in with his wife, so they could pretend it was just the two of them.

They both looked to the trooper hunched on the ground. "Use his radio. Call for help," Fen ordered. He crouched beside the ashen man, loosening the collar of his uniform, popping buttons to reveal a plain white undershirt. The man flopped back as Fen laid him gently in the dirt.

"What are you doing?"

"Call!"

She tiptoed to the police car awkwardly, trying both to hurry and to spare her feet. She slid into the seat and immediately felt claustrophobic with the monitor and CB radio and speed radar gun and clear plexiglass pressed up behind her head. She was afraid to touch anything, afraid not to when she thought of the trooper's eyes rolling back.

"Hello? Hello?" she said into the CB transmitter, pressing down on the side like it was a walkie-talkie. "Help?"

A reply crackled back. "Dispatch. Who is this, please?"

She explained that the trooper had collapsed "all on his own," that they didn't have cell service, that he needed an ambulance.

"What is your location?"

She panicked, tears sliding down her nose. "I don't know. We're in a cornfield."

"Ma'am, that's the whole county. I need you to be more specific. Where are you in relation to the city?"

"North. North of Lincoln, maybe five or ten miles? Not twenty, not that much."

"County road?"

"Probably?"

"Ma'am, is there anyone there with you, anyone who can help me pinpoint your location?"

"Fen!"

Turn-by-turn directions rolled from his mouth into the radio. Between Gunnar and SR 540, just east of Old Mill Road. And like that, help was on the way. Then Fen was back with the trooper, Marly staring at a tiny computer screen with his home address on it. She'd driven by. She'd never been inside.

She stepped lightly from the shelter of the police car into the cool wind. She stared at Fen rhythmically pumping the man's skinny white chest, the trooper's T-shirt torn to his throat where the banded collar still held. Fen tilting the man's head back into the dirt then seeming to kiss him fast and hard. She didn't know he knew CPR. She'd had no reason to. His hands fast and sure as they found the right place on the sternum and pressed again in a steady rhythm. She watched him listening to the heart and the lungs, repeating everything for several quiet minutes before the first flashing lights appeared like beacons from the south. She put on her shoes, the pressure making her wince.

First, all the questions. Then the praise, one EMT clapping Fen on the back and saying, "They'll call you a hero in the paper." The ambulance sped away, and the state police finished their report, a female trooper preparing to drive the other car back. Marly stopped her as she turned.

"Does he have kids?"

"Trooper Gibson's going to be fine," the woman reassured. "He was conscious when they took him."

"But does he have a family?"

The woman looked from Marly to Fen and back again. She smiled. "His first one's due in a few months. He'll be okay, thanks to you two."

As the last police car pulled into the country lane, Fen rubbed Marly's shoulder. "You don't think they'll really put this in the newspaper, do you? My name?"

"Hope not. Tough to explain band practice in the corn." Marly felt blood pooling between her toes, the stickiness in her underwear, the thick tender spot where she'd bitten her lip, the tears that kept welling and slipping through her lashes. *I'm leaking away*, she thought, sucking in one last deep breath of the dying countryside.

They drove back to the prairie city, him retelling the story of tearing the man's shirt and keeping his heart beating, his lungs full of air. She watched the light pollution increase, the tiny, stabbing stars fading.

"It's really late," she said. "Let's just drive to your house. I'll walk home from there."

"Are you crazy?"

"I mean you can drop me at the corner near your house." She wanted to see him turn the key, enter his front door, and close it again. She might be able to sleep then. But she couldn't say any of that.

"You *are* crazy. I wouldn't let you walk all that way at night for any reason, but with your feet all sliced up like that? What were you doing anyway?"

"Running."

"Obviously."

By the time they arrived at her apartment building, all she could pick out were the usual constellations, Orion and Ursa Major, Cassiopeia and Ursa Minor with the bright-burning, insistent North Star.

"I love you," Fen murmured, leaning in to kiss her. She turned her face.

"You've been smoking."

"You're just like my wife," he said, fumbling in his glove compartment for gum. The truck idled, the purr of an engine well-maintained.

"The peppermint flavor doesn't hide anything."

He slid off the wrapper and crammed the gum in his mouth. He kissed her anyway. She tasted smoke and mint and blood, her blood, in that mouth that could keep a stranger alive.

SCRAP MOON

7:18 a.m.

Outside on the patio where the other nurses gather to smoke, I sit down on a block of wood carved to look like a black bear, and I wish—not for the first time—that I was more like my son. The bear's nose, just inches from the ash can, is charred where the grown-up children of residents stub out their cigarettes. Anxious smokers, all of them, hurrying to get in, hurrying to get out, unlike the nurses who savor their breaks, pulling smoke from the smallest butts, holding it in their lungs until they can hold no longer. Then the nurses exhale.

On an ordinary day in Montana the brown haze is swept out by the blustering wind. Today is no ordinary day. Windless. The clouds of smoke cluster and hover, the stubborn ghosts of cigarettes. I wish I were like the other nurses, nicotine a reason to be out here every hour. I wish I were more like my son, his own life reason enough never to be where he doesn't want to be.

I am still looking for my reason, waiting for a wind, a warm chinook, to blow it my way.

8:42 a.m.

An acrid odor like urine or cleaning fluid. That smell is in my clothes and hair, and I think it would be better to be a smoker.

A bushy-browed man stubs out his cigarette on the bear's nose and rushes through the sliding doors. I must remember to move the ash can and spare the bear.

Gerta cries out for Jesus from the 100 wing. I can hear her through an open window. "Jesus! Oh, Jesus!" This is all she says, though sometimes she will say "thank you" when I bring a cup of tea. "Jesus, thank you. Jesus." Still, she can eat on her own. She doesn't need diapers. She never tries to escape. We keep her with the other independents and out of the 600 wing, the place for those with dementia.

My own mother tries to escape. She would join my son in Dallas if she could get that far. Three times a day the alarms blare from the 600 wing. One of the nurses out here, a smoker named Jeanette, always calls to tell me. This morning my mother cried, told everyone she'd lost me. So I finished after-breakfast meds and went for a visit.

"No," she said, "this is not *my* child. Lucy wears pigtails." My mother went off to search the other residents' rooms for wherever I was hiding.

"Ready to go back inside?" Jeanette asks, flicking her butt to the ground.

I never know how to answer.

10:16 a.m.

We are out for another breath of fresh air (carbon monoxide and toxic tar in Jeanette's case) when the bushy-browed visitor steps through the silent sweep of the electric doors. He stops to light up, then looks fiercely at us.

He points with his smoldering cigarette. "It's people like you," he says. "That's why I'm moving my father to the other place. More breaks than work. You just let people die."

He leaves. Jeanette lets her cigarette burn as she stares off after him and out to the open plain where not even a breeze rustles the short, brown grass. The fire hazard will be high this spring, summer even worse.

"He's right about the last part," she says. "That's Monty Messmore's son."

Monty is near comatose. Dying. We change him and spoon food into his mouth, all that's left to do now.

"Is he really moving his father to River Manor?"

Jeanette shakes her head. "He says he wants his father to be able to go on fishing trips like they do at the River."

I picture Monty Messmore in a wheelchair, rolled up to the bank, cap propped on his head, pole tied to his arm. A sunfish bites and it's enough to tumble his bony body into the shallow edge of the river. Five inches of water would drown him.

"Jesus," I mutter. Somewhere inside the home Gerta echoes me.

11:38 a.m.

Home for lunch and I find Charlie where I left him—in front of cable news reading the ticker aloud.

"A bus rollover in Virginia. Eight dead."

"Hello to you too."

Charlie was a high school guidance counselor who used to open the doors to new beginnings. Now, retired, he's obsessed with disastrous endings. An almanac of tragedy. If I tell him how a favorite resident died of pneumonia complications, he will give me the detailed story of Jim Henson's death: "He was still young. He had his whole life ahead of him. And he invented those Muppets." If I bring up the woman in her twenties, a quadriplegic the state gave us temporarily, he will tell me that she's lucky, that he saw a show about such a girl, only her family was *starving* her in a closet. Once, not long after the school year started without him, Charlie actually said, "I don't know how you stay in that job. Everyone just sitting around staring at television, waiting to die."

He turns from the TV and says, "Another actress dead of a heroin overdose."

"She's lucky," I say, searching for the sandwich meat. "She'll never grow old and end up alone."

"Is this about Dan again?" He leans out of his chair to see my face. I picture him toppling over. With his snack-cake belly, he might not get back up.

I was actually thinking of Katrina, a kind woman on my wing who loves birds and watches them at the feeder outside the picture window. Physically frail, she is still sharp-witted. Her husband is long dead, and she was an only child. Her only child lives in Brazil. When he tried to get her to move down, she said, "I'm too old to learn Portuguese." She said, "All my friends are here in Montana." But they are only buried here, under the short-grass plain. No one ever visits her, a shame because she loves to talk. When the nurses are too busy, she talks to the birds. Once, she tried to talk with Gerta but returned disgusted. "That woman is a proselytizer. At least Jesus *listens*."

"Why?" I ask. "Did Danny call?" He only calls during the day, when he can charge the bill to his workplace.

"No, but your father did."

"Is everything okay?"

"He caught a marlin. Well, with a lot of help. He's sending pictures."

My father lives with his girlfriend, a wealthy widow none of the family likes, in a retirement community in Florida. At eighty, he is still occasionally the rugged outdoorsman, the manicured golf course his adventurous standby.

Charlie calls for me to bring him a Coke, then says, "Your father invited Dan out there for a summer boating trip."

I look out the kitchen window where the crabapple tree is thinking about buds. The branches are perfectly still, like a photograph. Like we all exist in this snapshot, frozen, stuck, framed. I imagine my father on the prow of a fishing boat, gulf wind in his hair, most of which he still has. My son is beside him, pole out like a sword carving adventure into his future.

"I thought Danny couldn't get time off this summer. I thought that was his reason for not coming here." I open Charlie's Coke for him automatically, as if he were a child or elderly resident. I finish spreading the mustard on the sandwich I probably won't have time to eat on my short break.

"Who knows?" Charlie replies. "Wait, they're saying something about the dead actress." He turns up the volume. I watch a robin settle on a crabapple branch. I consider talking to it, telling it how a fish as big as a marlin could drown my father and my son in the deep ocean, how there would be no one to turn them over for another breath. *Take that message next time you fly south.*

Behind the bird and the tree, like a little scrape in the sky, is what my mother called a "scrap moon." A shade lighter than the clouds, just a withered hangnail, you hardly noticed it. Throwaway.

"They're saying that it might not have been an accident. Only the coroner can clear that up. Did you forget my Coke?"

I bring it to him. He takes it and drinks without so much as a thanks.

I sit to eat my lunch and Charlie turns the television to a different news channel where two guests are shouting at each other about Medicare policies. "Politics," he mutters, pressing the "go back" button on the remote. "Commercial breaks!" he pouts when the previous channel switches to an ad for supplemental life insurance.

"I was interested," I say. "We'll be old someday."

"Well, aren't you the cheery one?" Charlie says, punctuating with a small, satisfied burp.

12:30 p.m.

On my way back in, I notice the ash can is missing. Some really windy days it tips and rolls into the bushes. Now it is just gone, and the wooden black bear sniffs empty air.

2:12 p.m.

"Jesus!" Gerta is holding a one-woman revival. She rocks back and forth near the open window. "Jesus! Jesus!"

"I wish she'd fuckin' shut up," rasps an old man fumbling to light his cigarette. His fingers are swollen and twisted, arthritic. No one helps him. Once, he nearly lit up while his oxygen tank was still active. He doesn't remember to turn it off, so the director said no smoking. But George knows about patient rights. George called a lawyer, and now he's allowed as long as his tank is closed. But we aren't obligated to light cigarettes. Feed, wipe, and medicate, yes. Start a small fire? Not in the contract. So he works the slender lighter like someone wearing heavy work gloves. After five minutes, he is frustrated, near tears. He says it's the wind in his eyes. Today is windless.

Jeanette finishes her cigarette and heads inside. I pause. I have helped him before, after checking the valve on the tank. I do not want to end up in a thousand exploded bits, the smell of urine and smoke ushering me to the afterlife.

George looks up, shiny tears welling, but he doesn't ask for help. I shrug. "It's not good for you anyway."

"I want a smoke," he hollers. "A fuckin' smoke. It's my right!"

"Jesus!" cries Gerta.

"Jesus fuck!" George cries back.

"We don't always get what we want," I say patiently. "And stop with the curse words."

He tucks the cigarette and lighter back in his shirt, turns on the oxygen valve, and after a deep breath, says, "I got the right to curse. Consider yourself fucking sued."

4:00 p.m.

I've checked on my mother in her before-dinner nap, spittle pooling in the grooves of her cheek. The nurses say she misses me, but what am I to do when she doesn't believe I'm me? Outside, no need for a jacket, and most of the staff is there. Shift switch. One new nurse says she's got the rest of the week off to spend with her grandchildren who are visiting from Seattle. The wallets start to come out, the obligatory photo exchange.

I turn to sit on the bear and see that the ash can is back. "How did this get here?" I ask the oohing crowd. "Where was it before?"

Someone says that George had it. "He thought it was a spare oxygen tank." She shrugs. "I had to clean up the damn ashes."

"He didn't really think that," I say. "He's acting out."

"He's losing it," the nurse replies, then flashes a fake smile at someone's baby photo. "Have to send him to dementia one day." She says it like it's a destination. A trip to sunny Dementia.

I remember that the ash can was missing before my dispute with George. I'm as paranoid as the worst of them.

"Lucy, do you have grandkids?" The new nurse is offering me pictures, forcing them into my hands.

"No," I say. Then, blandly, "Oh, how cute."

"Kids?"

"Yes, a son."

"How old?"

This is the hard part, where the conversation always stutters: I say he is thirty-six, and the other person asks if he's married, and I say no, and she pauses like she wants to ask if he's gay. And I always wish he were then because it would be a reason, an explanation of why he stays so far away from this town.

I say, "Old enough to marry. It's only a matter of time. I expect an announcement any day."

This is a lie. The last time I asked him about marriage, Danny shouted into the phone. "Is that all you can think about? You, you, you." I wanted to repeat his words back to him, but I let him go off. "You want a grandchild. I want a life. I *have* a life. I *like* my life. I like the girls I date and the oyster bars where we meet and weekend trips to the coast. I don't want to be old before my time."

"So there's no one special?" I asked. "There are so many nice women in Montana. You should come up and look." He sighed and hung up, and I sat in my kitchen, wondering when it was time to be old.

Jeanette looks at me through a cloud of smoke and asks, "What kind of woman do you think he'll finally settle with?"

I choose another easy lie: "Someone just like me."

8:09 p.m.

When the phone rings, I nearly drop the plate I am rinsing. I am sure it is Danny, long overdue, and I think this time I might threaten to fly down there, see if that won't call his bluff. Charlie looks up from *The New Detectives,* where a murder victim, burned in a trailer, has just been identified by a single molar. Charlie likes tragedies with hard-won closure.

"Hello?"

LaDonna, the night nurse on the 600 wing, says, "Your mother won't settle down. She keeps getting out of bed to look for you. It's bothering the other residents, especially when she rummages through their drawers. Do you want me to give her a sedative? Or maybe you want to talk to her?"

Talking won't work. My voice will be a lie because now she's looking for an infant. My first cradle was a dresser drawer, and I swear the smell of cedar still makes me feel safe. My mother is searching for the child who needs her, depends only on her.

I can picture her lifting the corners of folded house-coats and underthings, expecting me. I can feel her fear when each time there is only another housecoat or the flat, hard bottom of the drawer. She is listening for my cry, her heart wild to find me and hold me tight.

By tomorrow, I will be neither pigtailed child nor dresser-drawer infant. I will be sucked back into her useless womb. She'll refuse certain foods, telling the nurses that her pregnancy makes her stomach sensitive. Then the egg and sperm will separate and go their own ways, absorbed into the body to drown. Alone. Like the hot spark when the oxygen is turned off, I will fizzle.

I look at my face reflected in the black kitchen window, shaky and unstable every time headlights on the street draw past. The scrap moon has long since set.

Sedate her. I almost say the words aloud. Then, "Put her on."

She says nothing, but I know when she's on the other end. Small gasps, like a tired wind, scuffle through the line. "Mama?"

Her breath, uneven, and nothing more. I listen to this lullaby.

SMOKE, IOWA

Deepest hue of indigo to the east, pale peach streaks on the western horizon. The low sun hanging round and hot like a promise that still appears full. Railroad tracks stretching from my vantage point in either direction, infinitely. Tracks long unused, overgrown with clover, ties splintered with rot.

She told me to pick a small midwestern town, to find the railroad tracks that are never far away. *Stand in the middle*, she whispered as she stroked the nape of my neck in a way that made all my skin tickle, like a thousand salmon brushing past on an urgent upstream journey. *Pretend you are the zero point on an infinite number line. To the west are all the negative numbers, to the east the positive numbers. That, my dear, is what forever feels like.*

She said that after we'd made love for the last time. I'd made the fatal error, the one I'm prone to make over and over. I'd asked if she would love me forever.

Women the world over ask that question, and I want to believe that most of them get the simplest answers: "yes" or "no." Or sometimes a hem and haw, which is the coward's tilt to "sorry, but no." I don't think any woman ever got the answer I did. And if so, I hope she chose tracks that were still in use.

Four months after she disappeared from my bedroom, I drove a short way out of the city. An hour or less. Smoke, Iowa. A nothing town like so many other places in middle America. I drove gravel roads until I found the tracks. I stepped from my car and stopped to breathe the air that hung thick with pollen and vegetable odor. But the air choked my lungs and tickled my sinuses, so I hurried to a sturdy tie in the center of the tracks.

I balanced, arms out the way I'd posed long ago on the balance beam in our elementary school playground. I'm a tall woman. I was a tall child. Sometimes I looked like a crane, elegant, posing for the still photographer. Other times I appeared gangly but earnest for takeoff. Those were always the times right before I overcompensated and landed in the dirt, a small puff of dust pressing out from beneath my sneakers.

I like to think I looked like a crane on this day.

Facing west, I studied the slow sink of sun, red and round as a perfect wound. Warm feathers of orange and pink bled into clouds that bled into sky. All that bleeding, endless. The ties on the tracks before me were notches, notches on the number line she told me about. But I couldn't remember whether they were positive or negative numbers. I still thought that mattered.

I turned east to where the earth and sky blurred in a swirl of navy and black. So dark I thought a storm was approaching until I remembered that weather moves west to east on the plain. That much I depend on, though always there are cyclones whirling every which way.

Still balancing on the railroad tie, remembering the only girl on the playground who could make me lose at "chicken" because she always looked me right in the eye, I heard a rumble like thunder from the west. I turned. I wavered on the beam.

A farm truck, aglow with the last of the sun, came crunching over gravel. I listened to it roar, then purr, then cut out altogether right beside my hatchback. The driver rolled down the window and ran her fingers through short, silvery bangs. She squinted, measuring me as I stood tall, an indivisible integer on an abandoned number line.

Finally she called to me: "You want a ride?" Her voice: rich, husky, the voice of a radio deejay or expert in phone sales, someone used to speaking mostly to herself, someone who enjoyed that.

I shouted that I had a car, and she laughed, the sound echoing back to me in a whirl of cricket song.

"That's not what I asked."

She shook her head. Then she gunned the engine and pulled away in a spray of gravel that pinged my car. I stepped off the railroad tie, scaring some small mammal back into the tall prairie grass, and I watched her go, that stranger who'd looked me in the eye and offered a ride. I could almost imagine the way that seat would smack my rear over every bump as we sped away from the zero where I'd planted myself, waiting for a nudge in the right direction.

I watched the taillights of that farm truck shrink until I could no longer see them. Still, I *had* seen them. I'd missed the moment the sun had plunged below the horizon, but I'd seen those small red lanterns, and I knew they still beamed at me from the dark. Whichever direction I turned, they would always flare, markers for where I'd never be.

THE SWEET AND
THE HEAT

The girl was alive. Elise knew without knowing, like those talk show psychics telling grieving parents half of what they want to hear: *alive*. Mothers gasped, their faces glinting under studio lights with hope and tears. Fathers bit their lips, leaned forward, their whole bodies wanting to believe. And then those psychics shook their heads so slow and sad. *That's all I can tell you*. Still those parents leaned forward in their seats, waiting for all the answers.

Elise carried that knowledge of a living girl like a seed that couldn't find fertile soil. Her own people had evolved in snow and ice and blackest nights extending for weeks. Just as her foremothers in their fur-lined hoods teetered toward the relentless seduction of melancholy, the sun returned, sparing all but the most desperate that descent into the dark self. The sun always returned. It seemed to bloom from the unturned snow, pale yellow bud opening every day more golden and alive.

To bloom. To open.

When dark nights in a soot-clotted city squeezed her, she told herself the flowering would come.

When the second baby dissolved into red river melt-off down her thighs, she told herself *snow blooms, snow blooms*. Repeated it like a mantra.

Levi said, "How fucking retarded." Levi said, "A woman doesn't need a brain to carry a baby. It's in her DNA. Even my ex could do that." The next morning, he brought cloying roses, their bloody petals drying brown. When she didn't smile in gratitude, he conceded, "I shouldn't have said 'fucking.'" Later, "Why do you always assume the worst, like I meant *you* were retarded? There was no subject in that sentence."

No subject. She thought about that a long time but couldn't remember how he'd phrased it. She arranged the roses in a vase. Forgot to add water. Cried when the petals fell. He said, "Baby, they start to die the second you cut them." But he held her, stroked her hair, and she clung to that like a branch that might, one day, burst forth with blossoms.

When Johnnie-Girl moved into the row house next door, Levi said, "That one's got bad news written all over her."

"Why?" Elise asked, but he didn't have an answer until they learned her name was Johnnie.

"Girl takes a guy's name—that says everything," he crowed.

"I took your name."

"Call yourself Levi now?" He laughed. "That's re-tarded." *He's dropped the cussing*, she thought. *He's trying*. But later, when she explained she was late with his pork chops because she'd taken a walnut coffee cake to Johnnie, he thought she meant his cousin, the one who made eyes at her. He threw a shoe so hard the plaster in the wall behind her chipped.

"No, Johnnie-*Girl*," she'd said, pointing next door. Then he laughed until his eyes welled with tears.

That's what they'd call her, he said, Johnnie-Girl.

"Are you sorry, then?" she asked, pointing to the mark. "For the wall?"

His eyes darkened. *Oh, Elise, don't push it.* "I'm sorry for the *shoe*," he said. Then, "Let's make a baby."

When her husband left for work, Elise walked the city, searching for Sharla. Even while running legitimate errands, she looked. She didn't tell Levi, didn't even speak his daughter's name anymore. "Dead to me," he said in a flat, chilly tone. Elise passed the houses on the slopes, imagining the girl curled up in some boy's bed, snoring softly and dreaming of horses. But, no, Sharla had loved horses when she was ten; now she was sixteen and wanted other things. Her note: *I want other things for myself.*

Sometimes all Elise wanted was to know what that meant.

In her dreams: Sharla at a bus station, her hair electric blue, new tattoos snaking her wrists. Boarding an impossible bus to Maui because all the laws of nature changed when Elise's eyes closed, the magician mind entertaining itself through the long night, manufacturing bouquets of tricks easily crushed when she remembered the word *impossible*.

I want other things for myself. What? But the dream girl would surf the bus into the ocean or liquefy and slip down a drain and Elise would wake, her chest thick with sorrow fresh as on that summer morning Sharla vanished from the real world.

They'd read the note, studied the emptied room for clues, and finally, in the sticky air on the small deck Levi had built with his own hands, animal sobs had burst from her, untamed pain that refused to back down when her husband shouted for her to stop, stop, stop.

"She's not even *your* daughter!" he shouted, running his hands through his thinning hair before clamping them to his ears.

That got through. The sounds from her gaping mouth withered, and she willed her selfish grief to end. He was the one suffering.

One morning she thought she spotted Sharla in the cultural district clutching a steaming cup of coffee with both hands to warm her fingers. Elise had crammed hers into her pockets to save them from the slicing wind. *She's dyed and cut her hair,* Elise noted. *In disguise.* But the familiar figure greeted her first, and she recognized her neighbor, Johnnie-Girl.

"That was the best coffee cake I've ever eaten," her neighbor said. "Wish I had some right now."

"I can give you the recipe."

"It's always better when someone makes it for you. Not that I'm asking. Just thanking you again for the lovely welcome." Johnnie-Girl smiled then, a dazzling smile that warmed the air. Her hair was so blond it was almost white, the roots dark like she'd planned it that way, all of it spiking up in tufts that looked soft as summer grass. She wore a red wool peacoat that, buttoned up, reminded Elise of Mickey Mouse's shorts.

"Funny you should say that," Johnnie-Girl said. "It's stolen from Disney World. Well, not exactly *stolen.* Part of the wardrobe. It was summer when I quit and everyone forgot about returning the coat, including me."

"The wardrobe?" She imagined Johnnie-Girl as a character cast member, a lively sprite like Tinker Bell or Peter Pan.

"I was a lifeguard. And before you ask, no, nobody ever drowns at Disney."

"I was going to ask why a lifeguard needed a wool coat."

A panel in the building behind them popped open, a plywood door that Elise hadn't noticed, and a man with a fake mustache drooping around his mouth crooked and wiggled his finger.

"Back to rehearsal," Johnnie-Girl announced, handing her empty cup to Elise. "See you in the 'hood."

Elise studied the lilac lipstick stain on the paper rim. Shimmering, like the pearly horns of the unicorn toys Sharla once collected. Elise carried the cup through the city, her fingers numb by the time she found a waste bin. When she looked back, a crow had already dragged the cup out and aside, searching for scraps.

The paralyzing snowstorm struck the next week. Five feet of wet and heavy snow. No one in the city could drive for days, not even the ambulance drivers who could navigate only the main arteries, all the connecting capillary roadways clogged with the snow that couldn't be pushed anywhere. One man died of a burst appendix, his wife calling 911 again and again while the EMTs waited one day and then the next on a street three blocks from his apartment. They wanted him to walk to the ambulance—it was only stomach pain—and, when he didn't, they drove away.

"Why didn't *they* walk to *him*?" Elise asked the droning television.

"Poor fucker," said Levi. He paced the room, restless without work to anchor him. "They should fire that worthless mayor."

"He didn't bring the snow."

"He didn't clear it either. City can't function for a week—it's the mayor's fault."

"It's always someone's fault, isn't it?"

Levi didn't answer.

That evening, as Elise thawed leftovers, their fresher food already gone, their car still walled with snow, the doorbell rang. Soon after, Levi came to the kitchen.

"Neighbor wants to know if we have eggs."

"Neighbor?"

"The boy-girl," he said, voice lowered. "Eggs."

"Johnnie? Of course." She wiped her hands on a towel and went to the refrigerator.

"I'll give them to her." He reached with thick, clumsy fingers.

Elise cradled the carton against her chest. "Where is she?"

"On the porch."

"It's freezing outside."

She went to the door and saw Johnnie on their stoop in her stolen coat, no hat or gloves, exhaling slow, frosty puffs, exaggerating the roll of her lips. "I could blow rings when I smoked," she said shyly. Snow clung to her coat where she'd pushed against the shrubs, forging a path between their houses.

"Come in," insisted Elise. She felt Levi's eyes boring into her back. "Hurry."

Johnnie didn't hesitate. She sprang across the threshold in a shower of snow and stood on the woven mat that absorbed snow and dirt and everything else that didn't belong in their house. It did not absorb Johnnie. If anything, she seemed larger and brighter in the foyer, her cheeks a jovial pink.

Elise shut the door with one hand, still clutching the eggs, and heard the floorboards creak, her disapproving husband returning to his television, stepping aside. For now.

"I was going to make cookies, just plain chocolate chip," Johnnie explained, "so it wouldn't be a terrible waste leaving the oven on. I thought I had everything I needed. And I didn't realize until the flour and baking soda were mixed and the butter and sugar creamed: no eggs."

"You need eggs." Elise handed the entire carton over.

"Just two."

"You might want to make something else. Who knows when this storm will get cleaned up?"

"Soon, I hope. Then I can get someone here to fix the furnace."

"You don't have heat?"

"That's why the oven is on." Johnnie grinned. "I sleep in the kitchen, in this coat. I pretend I'm a pioneer and that room is my whole cabin. Except I have modern plumbing and the outhouse is only a flight of stairs away. Which seems far in the middle of the night in a cold house."

"Stay awhile. Warm up. Do pioneers have neighbors? We can pretend the kitchen is my cabin. We can—I don't know—churn butter or trade beaver pelts."

Johnnie laughed, loud and confident. "That sounds dirty." Elise blushed. "But yes, I'd love to take off this coat. I worry it will meld to my skin and there I'll be, in sweltering August, still trying to shed it."

She hung her coat on a chair. She made a fuss over the pale green Depression-era glass on the shelves Levi had built for Elise's birthday one year. He'd mounted them high so their future children couldn't reach, and Elise had been touched by that detail. "My grandmother's," she explained. "I was the only granddaughter and inherited every piece because the boys said they didn't need dishes. There's more in a box in our attic."

"They're not just dishes!" The spiky ends of Johnnie's hair trembled with her passion. "They're pieces of your grandmother's soul. And valuable besides."

Elise smiled. She was tempted to lie, to tell a story of sitting in her grandmother's kitchen like they were doing now, maybe eating cookies off one of those plates, basking in love and adoration. But that grandmother had died before knowing she'd have any grandchildren to inherit her collection. The elders never addressed the cause of her death, and the nicest thing they had to say about her was that she kept an orderly house. Those pieces of her soul now gathered dust.

Elise checked on dinner and realized she'd forgotten to start the microwave. Ice crystals webbed carrots and potatoes and large chunks of beef into one unappetizing glob. She pressed *start*.

"What do you think it means if the nicest thing someone ever says about you is that you keep an orderly house?" she asked Johnnie as she boiled water for tea. Twenty-four-hour news droned from the other room, and she wished Levi would turn on music instead.

"That you're a badass bitch. Or so quiet nobody really knows you. Please tell me you aren't talking about yourself?" They both looked around the small kitchen with its clean, clutter-free counters, everything precisely in place.

Elise laughed. "No, my grandmother. Here, look." She swung open a low cabinet door to reveal a precarious tower of plastic containers that collapsed on cue, clattering to the floor. Two lids rolled in opposite directions and she caught them both, scooped all the pieces, and crammed them back on the shelf before quickly shutting the door. "See? Levi never opens these."

"Is he hard of hearing?" Johnnie asked.

"The volume *is* a little high." In the living room, the cable news commentators were no longer background noise. They argued loudly about the economy like boorish guests on her sofa.

Elise pulled two ceramic mugs with matching bowls from her cabinet and set them on the table.

"We're not using grandma's dishes?"

Elise paused to consider the row of cups and plates and dessert dishes, glacial green like something carved from ice.

"I've never used them."

"Are they sacred?"

"I'm not sure what that means."

"It's like something holy."

"I *know* what the word means. But I have no idea why they sit there every day, doing nothing but gathering dust. I don't know what *that* means."

"I bet they're gorgeous all lit up when the sun is out."

"The sun? What's that?" They both looked outside the window, a flat gray panel sometimes sparking with spits of snow. "Should we use them?"

"That's up to you. You could sell them on eBay for all I care." *Modest growth in stocks, but that doesn't account for*—Johnnie raised her voice. "He should get his hearing checked. Or maybe the volume control is broken?"

Elise smiled and nodded. She inhaled slowly through her nose, but it didn't help. Her chest tightened and her stomach began to swirl like a black hole opening inside her—*As if the free market can sustain itself without those extensive government regulations? Are you kidding?*

She spooned the beef stew into a bowl. Not beef, she imagined. Caribou, shot with her own arrow, the television a great howling blizzard outside. She handed the bowl, then a spoon, to Johnnie. She gestured for her to eat.

"I'll wait for you."

"Go ahead. Please. I'm a little nauseated." She sat and sipped her tea. She tried to concentrate as Johnnie explained how she wrote grants to keep the arts alive.

"Theater is on life support in this city," she said, her lips shiny with the juices of the stew.

"Everything is."

"What?" Johnnie cupped her hand behind her ear and leaned forward.

"Nothing." Elise smiled again, only it felt forced, like she was baring her teeth. Suddenly the room was silent, the television muted, and she felt even sicker. "Do you want to take that with you?"

"You kicking me out?" Johnnie glanced toward the living room then to her barely tasted stew.

"I need to cook for Levi."

"He can't cook for himself?" Johnnie's voice seemed thunderous in the quiet of the house.

Elise didn't answer. She cracked the cabinet with the Tupperware, fumbled for the first matching bowl and lid she could find, and sent her neighbor home with too much stew.

When Johnnie's red coat dimmed and disappeared in the swirling snow, Elise called her husband to the table. Then again. Louder, in case he'd fallen asleep, which he sometimes did and which, this time, she knew he hadn't. She ran warm water for the dishes. She sang soothing songs to the bubbles on her hands. She wished she were the kind of woman who wouldn't wait for whatever was to come, who didn't believe in "inevitable."

He was attentive and funny the next morning. He woke first and made the coffee. He shuffled a worn deck of cards and said he'd let her pick the game.

"I don't feel like playing," she said, wishing she could refuse the coffee too. He'd put just the right amount of sugar in, and she craved the sweet and the heat.

A cloud crossed his face, but he set his hand on her knee and said, "Look, we'll do whatever you want today. I'll probably be back to the shop tomorrow anyway."

"I want to get out of this house."

"Cabin fever, eh? I got it too. Sidewalk needs scooped again. Don't look at me like that. Wasn't saying you should do it."

Elise pushed back and stood. "I'll do it. You make lunch today."

"With what? No one's been to the store." He looked genuinely confused, and she fought the urge to give him ideas.

"Scrounge whatever you can find. That's what I've been doing."

They heard the snowplows as they ate canned black beans warmed in the microwave, sprinkled with garlic salt and pepper. Elise imagined fresh produce: sweet creamy bananas, the citric bite of an orange, crunchy apples and pears. Lettuce, crisp and green. Even the thought of tomatoes, so pink and tasteless this time of year, made her mouth water. Her fingers were stiff from the shovel and her too-thin gloves. They curled awkwardly around the spoon as she ate the lunch, which wasn't half bad. Maybe a little too garlicky, not that she'd say it aloud.

Levi was restless. Itchy without work to keep his hands occupied, but strangely happy. "Let's make a snowman," he suggested while lapping starchy purple sauce from his bowl like a little boy. "While we've got the time. Roads should be clear tomorrow."

"Where are they going to put all that snow?" She'd had to lift the shovel so high that her shoulders ached more than her lower back. If Levi hadn't shoveled twice during the storm, she wouldn't have made any progress.

"They've got dump trucks. They dump it outside the city."

She imagined the city sealed in snow, a fortress. A busy little city that had no idea what went on outside its walls, that didn't believe there *was* an "outside its walls."

"Let's make an escape tunnel in the backyard," she said. "We haven't even tried to open the back door."

"Now that could be fun," Levi said.

On the slopes where they lived, when the rains poured in spring, the water kept rolling past them, downhill, pooling in the street at the very bottom, sometimes flooding it. But the snow drifted against houses like thick frosting. The screen door pushed out, but try as they did, they couldn't move it. The screen sifted floury snow onto the floor, but the door stayed fast.

"There's no way out," Levi said, giving the screen a vicious kick before shutting the storm door.

Levi was called to work the next day. The essential streets and parking lots were cleared, and the city hoped to be back to business as usual. Elise pretended to be fast asleep that morning when he nudged her for a kiss goodbye. Then, when she heard the heavy front door slam, she fell back to sleep. She dreamed she was tunneling through the snow like a mole finding pockets of buried treasure. She woke huddled under the covers, reluctant to leave.

When she stepped out the front door to look at the tiny sun like a match lit in the sky, she noticed the Tupperware bowl at her feet. Inside, half a dozen misshapen cookies, crammed full of chocolate chips, melted together. Frozen in a state of melting. She brought the bowl inside, tucking it with the rest of the plasticware. Throughout the day she cracked the door, peeled back the lid, and nibbled on just one thawing cookie, trying to save the rest of them.

By afternoon, she was restless and curious about the city. She bundled up and, at first, wherever the sidewalks weren't clear, tried to step perfectly in other people's footprints. But the length of stride was always off, and she had solid boots. She stomped and plowed and kicked at the snow until she was breathless and smiling. She told herself she was wandering, just out for fresh air, but she ended up in the cultural district, circling the same block until she saw a familiar red peacoat.

"I thought you didn't smoke anymore," Elise teased.

"Hey!" Johnnie flicked her butt into a snowbank. She gestured to the two men beside her. "Rob and Bernie, lighting and props. Guys, this is my neighbor."

"Hi, Neighbor," one of them called.

"Do you want to see what I'm working on?" Johnnie asked.

"I've never been in a theater."

"What? You're joking. No? Then come into my world!"

The hidden panel revealed a backstage corridor. Elise followed Johnnie past the black walls hung with electrical cords and assorted props: tribal masks, empty picture frames, a musical triangle like the type she'd played in the third grade Christmas concert.

A beautiful, dark-haired woman in a tie-dye sweatshirt was alone on stage, flitting on her tiptoes and pausing in dramatic poses to deliver a line in her musical voice. Then she'd stop and curse quietly before starting over.

"I'm working on the most amazing dress for when she performs her dance in Act II. Silk crepe streamers on the skirt. Red and black. When she twirls herself dizzy, they'll lift up and blur." Johnnie closed her eyes like she could see the whole scene in her head.

"I thought you were stage manager."

"Costume design too. We're low budget."

They watched the woman alone on stage, lost in her solo rehearsal. Suddenly she turned and broke character, her tone weary. "J, I can't figure out how to exit this scene."

"I'm not the director!" Johnnie called. "Just get out without destroying everything I built." The actress gave her the finger, then morphed back into character, a swirl of energy among the props. At the door, Johnnie turned to Elise and said, "Wanna go home with me?" Then, "Not like that, Miss Priss. I'm done for the day. Wondered if you were walking back up to the 'hood."

"Eight. She was eight. Spray of freckles on her cheeks, gap between her front teeth, barrettes that never stayed in. And this sunny spirit that pulled people to her. But that changed as she got older. I guess that happens as you realize how you've been abandoned."

Elise invited Johnnie in because, while they walked, she'd asked what Elise was looking for. "Every step of the way you're scanning people's faces, peeking in alleys. Like you're in the witness protection program or something." And so she'd invited her in, wanting to confess.

"What do you mean 'abandoned'?"

"Her mom wasn't in her life. She left Levi and Sharla and moved south. Sends happy little postcards of oranges and palm trees every week, I guess."

"You guess?"

"Her dad's been saving them. To give her on her eighteenth birthday."

Johnnie's eyes widened. "She's never read them?"

Elise fought some flare of panic, pinching her fingernails into her leg until it passed. "I'm sure she's seen them," she said, and a thick silence descended like all those inches of snow dropping again and all at once.

Johnnie finally leaned back in her chair and propped a leg on one knee. "Can I say something?"

Elise stared at her and exhaled slowly. She picked up the last cookie on the plate she'd set out and took a vicious bite. Crumbs spilled to her lap. Her mouth full, she still managed to make herself clear: "No, you can't."

The sink sloshed with hot, sudsy water, her grand-mother's dessert plates stacked carefully on the counter. The sun was out, weak and more gray than yellow, but still out, struggling in the clouds, unfurling pale streamers through the thin film of grime on her window. She picked up the first plate, dunked it in the water, and with a fresh sponge slowly wiped it counterclockwise, turning it over, rubbing until the green was greener than she'd remembered. She held it up to the window. Rivulets ran down, tiny soap bubbles sliding in the wake. Glowing like a new leaf, the glass revealed its tiny imperfections and grainy shading. She held it higher to the light, and ticklish suds plopped on her forearm. Suddenly the plate wasn't there, and she heard more than saw it knock the faucet and carom to the floor. She wiped her hands on the nearest dish towel and retrieved it. The crack was straight and deep, edges fringed with spidery crackles. Something welled in her, that wild and panicky feeling, and she couldn't suppress it any longer. She held the plate out like it was the source of that terrible swell of pressure, and she flung it with muscle she didn't know she had into the far wall, where it left a mark but landed on the loveseat, somehow, impossibly, still intact.

Her heart beat fast and light in her chest, and she panted, breath tense and shallow. The drip from the faucet. Snow sliding down the roof. The throb of her heart in her ears. Nothing. No one was home, and nothing would happen. They were her plates anyway, hers to eat off or throw. She felt sorry for nothing but the poor wall.

Elise pulled the plug and let the hot, clean water surge down the drain. Wasteful, but she didn't care. Once Sharla—she must have been twelve or thirteen—had filled the bathtub to the top, and she'd emerged ten minutes later, radiating a clean, pink heat. Elise had scolded her for wasting water. "You say only ten minutes in the shower," Sharla had whined, tearful and confused. "But I'm supposed to take a *long* bath?"

Elise thought how sorry she'd been for yelling, but she'd said nothing because Levi told her children didn't respect apologies. "They have to know who's boss," he explained patiently when she'd wanted to follow Sharla to her room.

Johnnie answered on the first knock, and Elise saw disappointment flicker across her neighbor's face. "I'm sorry. Are you expecting someone?" Elise asked, shifting the small, heavy box in her arms.

"You say 'sorry' more than anyone I know. People will begin to doubt your sincerity. And yes, I'm waiting for the movers."

"Movers? You haven't been here more than a few months."

After peering down the street, Johnnie waved her in. "When opportunity knocks, you answer."

"I guess that makes me opportunity," Elise said, but her neighbor didn't seem to hear.

The house smelled of laundry soap and old wood, a pleasant combination that reminded Elise of her grandmother, the one she actually knew. Everyone described that one as "cheerful," a word that always made Elise suspicious. But Johnnie's living room was anything but cheerful. It was cold and empty except for a few packed boxes, a sleeping bag, and a small alarm clock, its dial glowing like a little moon.

"Are you moving in?" Johnnie pointed to the box.

Elise fumbled, suddenly ashamed. She shifted the box in her arms. "I came to ask if you wanted the dishes. These are the best pieces. I washed them, and you're right—they glow in the light now."

"You want to give me the best pieces of grandma's soul? I'm touched." Johnnie laughed. "But I don't need anything tying me down. If I ever had to flee in the night, well, I couldn't bear to leave behind the beautiful things I love. It's better not to have them at all." She smiled like it was some inside joke. "Do you have anything like that? Not your grandmother's dishes, obviously."

Sharla's face conjured in her mind. The little gap between her teeth, the way that gap revealed itself less often over time, those sunny smiles growing rare until the girl was gone, just gone. But still alive, she reminded herself. Wasn't there always a bright side? A glimmer?

"Not these dishes, no. But I do need to set them down for a bit."

"Set them down for good for all I care. The owner of the house can have them instead of the rent I haven't paid." Johnnie chewed on her thumbnail, then blew on her hands to warm them.

Elise crouched and slid the box from her aching arms to the floor. "You're leaving?" She hated how those three syllables sounded: needy, desperate, clingy.

"One way or another," Johnnie said. "Those guys were supposed to be here by now. But I've got two good arms and money for a cab."

They both glanced to the alarm clock. Its silvery glow webbed the wall. Elise squinted to see the hands and realized that it was past time for Levi to be home. She whirled to the door in automatic panic. A sudden knock froze her in place. She turned back, eyes wide, hand hovering, fingers trembling.

Johnnie's eyes met hers. Cool and steady, like she was silently saying, *You got this.* Anyone could be standing on the other side. Levi, his face coiled in anger. Burly men ready to carry Elise's only friend to another life. A child starving for love, this time meaning to stay.

The trick, Elise thought, was to open that door like she wanted whatever was coming.

PARTING GIFTS

The only word she can remember is *jī*. She abandoned her vegetarian ways for *jī*, for the simplicity of confident ordering in those crowded restaurants ripe with the scents of Szechuan spices and body odor that smelled earthy and clean, never unpleasant.

The flight attendant smiles, then asks something in Mandarin, but Amy shakes her head, shrugs. Smooth switch into elegant, formal English then. "Would you like rice or potato with that chicken?"

"Oh, potato. Definitely potato." Six weeks in Chengdu, and now she's even forgotten the word for rice, a willful blot of memory considering she ate it twice a day. In week three, she'd started craving American movie theater popcorn, especially that oozing, unnaturally golden, butter flavoring. She would shovel rice in her mouth between classes and imagine the sauce was butter, sometimes creamy with fat, sometimes thin and chemical.

When she lands in San Francisco, she will find a snack kiosk, buy a small bag of stale popcorn for breakfast, drench it in fake butter and shamelessly lap the drippings from her fingers. For now, potato and the small square of what she hopes is real butter. The woman in the navy suit and silk scarf printed with tiny wings hands her a foil-topped box and a wrapped pack of utensils that Amy punctures with her nails, shredding the plastic to get to the fork. But as soon as she stabs at the chicken breast, the tip of a tine snaps off, springing over to land on the tray of her neighbor, the woman in the middle seat who doesn't like her, who is eating pork and rice or, rather, digging in the small purse tucked in her lap, ignoring her lunch. The woman hasn't seen the plastic shard land in her rice, and now it is lost, a tiny bit of white in a hundred tiny bits of white.

Amy pauses. Her only Mandarin is *jī* and *xiè xie*, neither of which is useful now. She gently taps the woman's forearm and points to her plate. The woman looks surprised, but she has looked that way since they boarded, her eyebrows plucked and redrawn into severe arches. Earlier, when she was speaking rapidly and, Amy presumed, angrily about her to the flight attendant, the effect of those brows made it seem she'd suffered some outrageous shock and not just the bad fortune of a seat in the middle, two rows from her husband.

The woman stares at Amy, who gestures to the broken end of her fork and then to the woman's rice. Still staring, the woman speaks machine-gun Mandarin, clipping the words, rapid-fire, until the passengers around them also stare at Amy. Again.

"You take her husband's seat and now you want her lunch?" An elderly man in a golf shirt behind her clicks his tongue in disgust. He speaks to the surprise-eyed woman in her language, sparking some new diatribe that Amy cannot understand.

"*My* seat!" Amy reminds them. "This has always been my seat." She thought this argument was settled, but now, two hours later, her troubles are back, all because she is trying to keep a woman from ingesting plastic.

"Is there a problem?" Another flight attendant sweeps into their section of the cabin, someone new who wears her scarf with the tiny wings like a wrap holding back her long hair. But before Amy can explain, the other woman starts gesturing, her whole body an argument. The attendant stops her, then leans in and asks if Amy would like her own plate of rice.

"No!" Now the flight attendant's eyebrows rise in surprise, settling quickly into a cool look she'd give a misbehaving child. "I'm sorry," Amy says, "but I'm only trying to tell her that part of my fork broke and flew into her food." She holds up the fork for everyone to inspect, pushing her own finger painfully against the jagged edge.

The attendant and the woman exchange more words, but the woman seems more outraged than before, pointing at Amy with a bony finger, nail bitten to the quick.

"She says you're sitting in her husband's seat?"

"That's not true."

"Could I see your boarding pass?"

Amy, grateful she crammed it into the easily accessible seat pocket after the first argument, hands it triumphantly to the flight attendant, who glances at it and nods. Her tone is more stern when she talks to the woman. "I paid extra for the leg room in this row," Amy adds, feeling finally that someone understands. "My circulation isn't good."

Then her neighbor bursts into tears, wailing so that all the flight attendants serving lunch and beverages swivel to look. A man a few rows behind them calls to her, repeating the same syllables over and over in a soothing, steady voice. Her name? Amy doesn't know. The flight attendant speaks to the woman while Amy focuses on slow, steady breaths and flexes her calves, one leg extended into the aisle.

"You can say no," the flight attendant begins, turning to her, "but this couple is only wondering if you'll switch seats so they can sit together."

"I know," Amy says. "They asked at the start of the flight."

The attendant nods. Her eyes are large, a gentle, honeyed shade of brown. "I understand. It's just, well, they're on their way to retrieve their son's body from the U.S. Their only child. Mrs. Yang needs some extra support right now."

Amy sighs, her legs suddenly prickling with restless pain. "Tell her I'm so sorry to hear that. But I paid extra," she mumbles, and the flight attendant says something to the woman, who weeps more quietly now. She pats the woman's shoulder and moves on to distribute bottles of water. Amy turns her body away from the grieving Mrs. Yang, but she worries the other passengers are staring, condemning her, so she fumbles in her bag for her sleep mask.

At the university, they called it an immersion program. Amy didn't need to speak Mandarin because the students were expected to practice English. When one young woman asked how many children she had, she said, "None." The faces of the female students slackened with such sorrow that she assumed they'd misunderstood. "Zero," she said. "I don't have children." They mumbled apologies to her, bowing their heads. "No, it's okay. If I had them, I wouldn't be here meeting you!"

Their expressions changed slightly, allowing now for the possibility that this American, who lived in a world where she could have all the babies she wanted but claimed to prefer teaching, was demented. "Does your husband want children?" one bold young man asked. She paused.

"He did," she admitted. "And now he has them with his second wife. Whatever." The students bowed their heads to whisper translations to each other.

One asked, "What is *whatever*?"

Amy stared up at the ceiling as she always did when figuring how to best explain those words and phrases she took for granted. "It means no big deal." Blank looks, and half the class bent to use the translator on their phones. "Um, just that something doesn't really matter. It's not important. A little thing."

Finally, the one who'd first asked about children, the one who called herself Miley after an American pop star, asked, "I'm sorry, but I'm confused about *second* wife. You are a first wife, then?"

She recognized how she might eliminate confusion by explaining she meant he was an ex-husband, she now the ex-wife, but she nodded. Better being first.

The day before Amy was to return to the States, Miley gave her a parting gift, a bracelet carved from yak bone. "For luck," she said.

"Luck? Really?" The tiny skull-shaped beads seemed ominous.

Miley laughed. "In China we say every gift is for luck. But this is from Tibet so maybe this is healing, maybe peace?" She shrugged. "It's a gift. *Whatever*."

She wakes from her nap. Her mask has slipped askew, and she's confused by the blurry ball glowing hot pink outside the plane's window until she understands it is the morning sun just emerging on the horizon, stunning at 40,000 feet. She finds her cell phone and leans across the sleeping woman beside her to capture the image, careful not to touch her. She pauses, studying Mrs. Yang's slack mouth and those dark arcs over her eyes that draw attention away from the subtler dark circles under them. Then Amy reaches out. She shakes her arm gently, watching the woman's eyes flutter and struggle to focus.

"See the sun?" Amy asks. She points out the window, beyond the young man sleeping in the window seat. Amy still doesn't understand why no one asked *him* to change seats. The woman leans forward to look and the now scarlet sun casts a rosy glow over her.

Mrs. Yang calls over her shoulder, twisting in her seat, and her husband creeps up with a camera, as if he's been alert and waiting for this moment. When he gestures politely, waiting for Amy's invitation to squeeze past her seat to take a picture, she stands in surrender. *Xiè xie,* he repeats. *Xiè xie.*

She walks the aisle in her displacement, long, unnatural strides to stretch her calves. But no one stares at her. The passengers who are awake all lean toward the sun, faces bright as the newly born.

TO TASTE

The baker's daughter steals her daily bread, tucking rolls and warm crusts in her skirt. She nibbles these as she walks to school some misty mornings. Sourdough is for the sea, for boats to weather any storm and gulls to guide her home. Honey wheat is for the plains, the dirt she would plough, the farmer's wife she could be. The croissants are for Paris, for silver jets and open-air cafés, for the way she will let strangers kiss her. Her pockets, stained with butter, become translucent as the skin of saints.

She grows fat on bread, her arms resembling loaves tucked and pinched and rising up out of the pan. Her mother complains, What boy will love you now? She moves the butter, hides the cheese, forbids whole milk, and locks up the cakes. The baker's daughter simply smiles, shaking out the telltale crumbs on her return so the sparrows can imagine they're gulls, so the starlings can dive with the red-tailed hawks.

One day while she lets Paris melt in her mouth, tasting *joie de vivre* on her tongue, she steps into a city street and the milk truck can't stop. Her spirit rises like good yeast, and a grackle steals the bread that falls, cold, from her hand.

The milkman is horrified, the mother distraught, and the baker throws his starter doughs into the trash. A starving woman rooting for a meal will find it and eat it and feel her stomach expand with cramps for days.

The milkman brings to the silent bakery bottles of milk, their necks clogged with cream thick and white as snow. He begs the baker and his wife to taste. His eyes fill with tears, and while the baker turns away to dismantle his mixer, his oven, his life, his wife stretches her finger and takes a small taste.

Each day the milkman returns. Each day she drinks more until one morning she gulps a whole bottle and milk spills down her chin and onto her breast, where it stains and sours by nightfall. The baker tells her to throw away that dress that smells like the infant their daughter once was. But his wife wears the dress to bed and in the morning when the new milk comes. Their bed begins to stink.

She grows fat with milk. Her breasts swell and her hips round as they did when she was with child. The milkman sees how lovely she is, milkfed. He imagines her on his dairy farm, kneading bread and feeding children, lots of plump, healthy children.

And because her fingers still remember the roll of dough and her breasts the pull of milk, she leaves with the milkman and buys a new dress, white as cream, silky as flour. They honeymoon in Paris, they make love by the sea, and they raise their babies on whole milk and cheese and buttery croissants.

One winter day, when a thin man steals from their trash a crust of bread, he will chew it slowly and recognize the taste. He will imagine he is a sailor facing the salty spray, or a farmer cutting the earth. Finally, at night, stirring the molding blankets of his bed under the pier, he will remember that once he baked. Once he made everything rise.

WINGS AND OTHER THINGS

She thought she was haunted: that shudder echoing through the living room's west wall like the bass line to her favorite show's theme song. When she muted the TV, nothing but the wind chimes on the porch clinking offbeat. Then the sound again, pinpointed now to the fireplace. Stupid, loose damper rocking with the draft. Anya twirled the knob, and it spun freely, catching on nothing, doing nothing. Stupid, hand-me-down house.

Then she recognized the sound as wings stirring air, a soft, flapping smack on brick. She hopped back from the fireplace and crouched as if something were about to erupt, horror-movie style—the cave flooding with bats, the attic a tornado of sharp-billed crows. She froze in her ridiculous pose, barely breathing and embarrassed, though she had no audience.

Her Pittsburgh grandmother would say, *Bird in the house means death.* Her Morgantown grandmother would say, *Angels come in all disguises*. Jason, if he were still around, would say, *Babe, it's just a bird. It won't hurt you.*

That man could take care of any problem, even when she didn't like the solution. Problem: losing his job when Halliburton pulled out, capping the local gas wells. Solution: following the work to North Dakota, leaving her behind. Her Pittsburgh grandmother had said, "You don't let a good man go." Her Morgantown grandmother had said, "When God closes one door, he opens a window."

Right then everything was open. The chimney, the flue, the fireplace, the possibility that anything could fly in her face.

The fluttering continued the next morning, and Anya's spine crawled to hear it. She avoided the living room and silenced the radio so she could hear if the bird left. But what sound does leaving make? With Jason, it had been the damaged muffler of his truck. But that, too, had been the sound of his arrival.

What if the bird were injured? Trapped on a small ledge and yearning for the postage stamp of blue sky visible. Flapping her wings for takeoff and going nowhere. What if the bird fell into the fireplace, panicked wings scattering ash?

Anya's stomach clenched. She gathered duct tape and a thick, black plastic garbage bag. She quickly sealed the fireplace, steeling herself when the beating wings resumed. The final strip of tape pressed into place, she felt relief, her world contained again.

That evening, after her shift at the sports bar, Anya settled into an armchair to unwind with a magazine, the type that told her how to pluck her eyebrows and keep a man. Her throat convulsed when she heard the crinkling of the plastic bag over her fireplace, followed by a small whoosh. The bag was moving, and Anya jerked out of her seat. But it was the wind. Of course, the wind. The draft sucking the bag back, then expanding it again, like a dark lung, the house breathing.

◆◆◆

In the morning, the sound—again—of wings in too-small spaces.

Two chimney service companies in town, and the first one wouldn't help. The woman on the other end said, "Bird? It'll fly out on its own."

"What if it's hurt?" Anya asked. "I've heard it for days now."

"Could be nesting then."

"No. The flue is open. The damper is broken. I can't have baby birds falling into my fireplace." She imagined the blind, bulge-eyed, featherless things squirming and choking in the thick layer of ash she failed to clean after winter.

"We aren't a wildlife removal service."

Anya huffed. "I need my chimney cleaned. Can you do that?"

"Not if those birds are chimney swifts."

"Why not?"

"Migratory Bird Act. They're protected." She heard the flutter-shudder again, like muted applause, and Anya hung up.

Remember, the web page advised, *the birds are more frightened than you are*. But that wasn't true, not yet. The birds were building a home, oblivious to Anya's intentions. The garbage bag sucked in, billowed out. The fluttering filled her ears.

Chimney swifts once nested in tall trees, but as the trees disappeared, they adapted to open chimneys. Now, with redesigned chimneys, most of them capped, nesting sites are limited, and the chimney swifts' habitat is again threatened.

She called Jason that night. "How's North Dakota?"

"Hey," he said, voice soft and—she hoped—lonely. "You remembered my number. You still mad?"

"I was never mad," she answered, deciding it was true. "It's just—you're forever away now."

"Not forever. Just until the work ends."

"And then what?"

He paused so long that she rushed to fill the space with her bird woes, telling him about the damper and the horrible, trapped fluttering sound.

"It's always something with that house," Jason said. "Sell it. Move here." And then she *was* mad because the market was flooded with houses since the oil and gas company pulled out, realty signs popping up on lawns like stubborn weeds. Even if she wanted to live in North Fucking Dakota, no one was going to buy this house, certainly not those squatting, seasonal birds.

"I want a *solution*, Jason. Not some pipe dream."

"Pipe dream. That's funny," he said. "Because of the gas pipeline. I'm literally following a pipe dream, yeah?"

She hung up on someone for the second time that week, swirling with a childish rage, embarrassed, and angrier for it.

Rainstorms the next morning, and Anya was happy to go to work. The damn birds would be staying in, and she didn't want to hear them.

"I should have been a nurse," she told Becky, the bartender, as she straightened the same stack of napkins again. "No shortage of business there." Slow day, only a few local attorneys and court clerks out for lunch.

Becky admired her own perfectly polished nails, waving the tips of her fingers like casting a spell. She splurged on a weekly manicure and a monthly massage in Pittsburgh. Her boyfriend, who worked in the lab at the hospital, was the only local Anya knew who wasn't perpetually underemployed.

"So go back to school and be a nurse."

"I don't like blood."

"Nobody *likes* blood. Except vampires, I suppose."

"I faint when I see it. And I don't handle suffering well."

Becky laughed and shook her head. "Oh dear," she said. "This is about Jason, isn't it?" Becky wandered to the far end of the bar, posing her rose-colored fingernails against the ruby swizzle sticks, then the orange and lemon wedges. "Sweetie," she called, "move there or move on!"

On one of their first dates, Jason had taken her for a walk in the woods. He'd grown up on the Maryland/ West Virginia border, a nature boy to the core, and hand in hand they'd stood by a small creek that babbled as steadily as she did. She was in the middle of some story, about the coal trains that shuttled through the center of town in the night, when he let go of her hand and squatted by the bank, eyes fixed on a rock that turned out to be the tiniest turtle she'd ever seen, its shell smaller than a quarter. Jason pinched it gently in his fingers and held it up so she could see its long tail flicking, miniscule jaws snapping as its head turned back and forth. It looked like a wind-up toy, head and tail jerking, tiny block feet paddling the air.

"Even the babies are mean bastards," he noted with an admiring laugh. He held the turtle to his face. "Fight on, little snapper," he whispered, and he set it in the grass, away from the bike path. They watched it turn like a slow, jerky clock hand and move stubbornly toward the dry, gravel path. Jason picked the turtle up again and carried it to a flat, sun-warmed rock beside the creek. "Stay," he ordered.

She'd really started to like him then, this savior of small creatures. They walked back to the car, and she tried not to talk too much, listening instead to the calls of birds she'd once been able to name. She inhaled the heady honeysuckle punctured with acrid pockets of natural gas.

When Anya returned from work early because there hadn't been enough for her to do, she called the second chimney servicing company. She said, "I want to schedule my annual cleaning now, get it done before fall."

They came the next morning in a white van fitted with extending ladders, crammed with buckets and brushes and tools. Two men carried into her living room large canvas tarps, a super-sized shop vacuum, and various rods and brush attachments. The short, thin one greeted her and introduced himself—Roger—and his partner, Gary, a large, silent, bearded man who nodded acknowledgment and methodically unfolded the tarp around the opening of her fireplace. Anya held her breath, expecting the fluttering-shuddering, but all was quiet. Maybe the bird really had left. She hadn't had her fireplace cleaned since she'd inherited the house, so not all was lost.

"What's this?" Roger asked, pointing to the garbage bag taped so precisely to the brick.

"Drafts," she said. "My flue stays open."

"I can check that." He peeled the tape and pulled back the bag, and Anya tensed. "Tall as this chimney is, we're going to clean from the inside," Roger explained.

"Don't you have an orphan to do that?" she murmured, watching Gary, the silent one, connect rods.

Roger laughed then asked, "Do you have any idea how many of those kids back in the day died of scrotum cancer?"

It wasn't the sort of question to which one had an answer, though Anya had a good guess as to how many of the men who worked the coal mines when they were open had perished from lung disease. Like her father, dying slowly and painfully years after his last company paycheck. Her Pittsburgh grandmother had said, "The wages of sin is death." Her Morgantown grandmother had said, "My son was a cheater, yes, and your mother deserved better, but he worked hard, Anya. He took care of you."

"We'll start with this mess," Roger advised, picking charred chunks of log from the grate and tossing them into a blackened bucket. "Whoa, look at this." He pulled from the ashes a small, dark bird, dead. He held it by a wingtip so one wing fanned open. Anya stared. She'd never imagined a bird already buried in the graveyard of her neglected fireplace. He flicked the body into the ash bucket and said, "You might have a nest." He flipped the vacuum switch, sweeping the open hose back and forth until the bottom of her fireplace revealed its flat, stone floor. "Don't worry," Roger said. "This thing will scare any remaining birds right out." He brandished a stiff black brush the size of a basketball, spidery legs in all directions.

Anya moved to the far end of the living room, feeling dizzy like the room was devoid of oxygen. How long had the corpse lain there? Not long, she reasoned. She was sensitive to foul smells. She shivered. *Goose walk over your grave?* Both of her grandmothers liked that one.

The vacuum droned again, and she moved outside where the sun was burning off the dew, warming the last puddles from yesterday's rain. She shaded her eyes with her hand and studied her chimney. It looked almost flat, two-dimensional against the sky's uniform blue. While she waited, hoping to see something fly out and away, silhouettes of birds sailed through the blue, some robins, a couple crows, and dozens of chimney swifts with their telltale angled wings. She knew what nested in her own open chimney, and she felt sick again with guilt and anger and who knew what else.

Her father had been a bird-lover. When she was twelve and was assigned a bird identification project in Life Science, he'd taken her out in the forests and fields with binoculars and a guidebook. Her parents had split by then, and he was living in the house that was now hers, dating a mostly sweet, alcoholic woman and working for PennDOT. "Nobody's going to shut down the highways," he reasoned, keeping that job until full-time use of an oxygen tank forced his retirement. Anya marveled how by summer's end his skin turned nut-brown, almost as dark as her shadowy memories of him when he'd come home in the morning from the mine, face washed, neck and ears still black until he'd shower.

She couldn't remember all the birds they'd identified that spring, but she'd finished with a perfect score on her project and a sense of wonder for all the creatures she'd never noticed nesting in thickets and the crevices of dead trees.

Something black popped up from her chimney, but it was only the large, round brush, bobbling, then flopping over the brick lip as someone fed it more line. Gary appeared in her doorway and spoke for the first time. "Is it out?" His voice was deep and loud.

She didn't know if he meant the bird or the brush, but she nodded. He signaled Roger, and the brush slowly retracted, then suddenly disappeared like a threatened creature retreating into its burrow.

Anya's return to the house was unhurried, a lingering in the late spring air. She studied the dirt patches where her mother, who'd remarried and moved to Delaware, had once planted cheery, colorful annuals. "Move out here," her mother suggested when they talked on the phone. "Try it for the summer. All the bars and restaurants near the beach are hiring." Once, when Anya had begun her rebuttal with the words "But the house," her usually agreeable mother had snapped, "Screw that house."

Anya paused on the wide porch, noticing the buckle and curl of peeling paint, then crossed the threshold. The men were retracting the brush, pulling hand over hand, speculating about hockey playoffs, when something burst from the fireplace. The men ducked and Anya screamed like a demon pursued her. She fled through the front door, not stopping until she reached the curb, hand on her chest, breath hitching. She knew, consciously, that it was only the dead bird's mate, and she felt like a fool, but her legs locked and she stood paralyzed.

Roger appeared in the doorway, gingerly carrying a folded piece of canvas cloth. He walked purposefully toward her driveway, away from where she trembled, and he squatted and let the folded cloth fall away. The dark gray bird paused briefly to orient herself, then took off, wings flapping hard, straight down the street as if navigating a map. They watched her flap and flap, then shrink until she disappeared.

Roger smiled. "Stubborn bird. Stayed in the nest all that time, but we scrub the walls on the way down."

"Nest?" Anya echoed. Comforting word, but all it conjured was painful longing in her chest.

"Gary's taken care of it. Shit, which one of us screamed anyway?" he teased. She blushed, and he said, "No, don't be embarrassed. Things hit us in ways we never expect. Like that movie *Titanic*. When I left the theater, I was crying too hard to see. My wife drove us home. She never said a word about it either. Just kept her hand on my back all night."

Anya looked at his face gone soft with memory, and a sob erupted from deep in her chest. Sudden, bewildering tears. Roger's eyes widened, but she held up a hand. "I'll be fine. We'll all be fine." And she rushed, half-blind, into the house to find her checkbook.

While she waited for Roger to finish writing her bill, she pressed the meat of her palms to her eyes and asked what to do if the bird came back.

"It won't," he said. "It might return to check on the nest, but the mate's dead, and the nest isn't there. No reason to stay."

"Isn't it, uh, illegal to remove the nest of a chimney swift?"

He paused with his pen poised as if writing on air. "Do you want me to put it back?"

When Anya was a girl, when her father still lived in the house with them, they'd had a black, plastic, wall-mounted phone. When she was home alone, her father hundreds of feet below ground, her mother cruising the grocery aisles, coupons clutched in her fist, Anya liked to call her own number and listen, the receiver pressed to her ear until the skin throbbed, hot and sticky. Self-hypnosis. That incessant, rhythmic busy signal, pulsing, calming her, reminding her that somebody was home. She'd tried it again after her father's death, the landline long gone, but her cell phone offered only a manufactured voice asking for a password to let her hear messages she knew didn't exist.

Anya signed her check with the big loopy letters she hadn't used since she was a teenager. "Fixed your damper," Roger remembered as his partner carried the ash bucket with the dead bird out the door. "Let me show you."

She peered up the chimney while he pointed out the mechanical gears, the teeth that had been off track, unable to grab on and rotate the damper. "Which," Roger added, "was somehow flipped upside down. But now, when the knob's in this position, you've got a good seal. Nothing's getting in."

She didn't ask about the nest, whether there were eggs. She hadn't heard peeps or any sounds beyond those fluttering wings, but who could detect the throb of tiny avian hearts in their shells? Now it was all she heard. Like a rapid drum line at a football game across town. Or a ceremonial summons from a faraway tribe. The ocean beating the Delaware shore, the rhythmic muffler blasts on a truck a thousand miles west. Always at a distance, those calls of life. When they came too close, wings and other things in her walls, she got someone else to answer.

BIG SKY BLUE

My mother wouldn't let me wear white. She had her suspicions, and how could I argue when I knew my guilt? We told the rest of the family that the apple-green silk went best with my coloring, and only my mother and I knew about the worm in the apple. The others might have suspected something, rushed plans and all, and I figured I'd have to tell them once I started showing, but all of us—Mother, Scott, and me—wanted the wedding to be tasteful and free of nasty gossip.

While they privately fretted over how an airman's salary could support a wife and child, I worried over another possibility, that we'd all be transferred to another air base. I knew that my intended didn't much like Great Falls, but there were worse places, I assured him. He usually agreed with me, citing high school buddies who'd ended up in North Dakota, but when the winds blew fifty miles an hour in freezing temperatures and he had to run drills out in the field, Scott cursed this place.

He wanted to be closer to his family in Texas. He was just two years out of high school and lonely for the desert and his friends and his mama's barbecued chicken. He cried once to me, drunk on whiskey, about all these things, and I almost believed that the force of his sadness could bend the military to his wishes. He'd whisk me away to unknown territory, a land of scorpions, separating me from my parents, my younger sister, Edith, who I adored, and all the scattered cousins and relatives in Butte and Helena. I'd only known Scott for five months, and most girls in my position were looking for exactly what I feared: a ticket out of Great Falls, Montana. That's why my high school friends flirted with the air force men they'd see at the Woolworth's lunch counter or Tracy's downtown. The thrill of travel, the security of government benefits—they wanted these things. But I was only eighteen and, despite my excitement at all the change on the horizon, afraid.

"A married woman!" Edith whispered, her bright eyes flashing as she French braided my hair the morning of the wedding. "My sister will be a married woman. That's practically the same as being old." She pulled my hair a little harder when I tried to punch her, and I glared at her, though secretly I loved the attention. Edith was only fifteen, not even old enough to date by our family's rules, so everything I did with a boy was as thrilling to her as Peyton Place.

My obvious choice for maid of honor, she was taking the role seriously. The wedding shower was small but splendid. Edith had borrowed recipes from her home economics teachers and made beef brisket and sugar mints for my friends and aunts. She'd bought the ingredients with money saved from her job in the church nursery. I knew she'd been saving for something special like a prom dress, and then she chose to spend it on me. She'd flat refused to play the silly kitchen appliance games suggested to her by my cousins. Edith had style. She checked out books on home decorating and cooking from the public library. She fingered the expensive silks at the fabric store and tried not to seem disappointed in the cheap dress I bought her. Mother warned her not to put on airs, but she said she was going to be somebody. Mother told her she already was somebody, but that only made my sister laugh, scornful at such a young age. Sometimes I'm surprised that Edith didn't marry military, but she wouldn't have been satisfied with anything less than an officer, and those were hard to come by.

"Do you think things will change with us when I'm married?" I asked, suckling my pinky where I'd worried the skin with my teeth until it bled. It was a horrible habit, one I only indulged when I was especially anxious. Edith slapped at my hand and held a tissue to the tiny cut.

"No," she said. "Except we'll probably stop fighting over space in the bedroom." I needed to hear that because all the evening before I'd moped about moving on base. Scott had reserved a two-bedroom duplex apartment for us. I'd only seen it from the outside because he said he wanted to surprise me.

"There. You look beautiful." She finished tying the green ribbon at the end of my short braid, and we looked at ourselves in the dresser mirror we'd cracked three years earlier while trying to juggle bottles of nail polish we'd stolen from the five and dime.

"Mirror, mirror on the wall . . ." I began.

"Who's the fairest of them all?" Edith finished in a nasal voice that always made me laugh. We locked eyes, half-smiles on our faces until Edith grumbled. "Oh, I'll give it to you this time. You're the bride after all." I pretended to gratefully accept the crown, though we both knew I would have won on any day. I had what my aunts called a "country rose" look: light brown, wavy hair, eyes the color of cornflowers, pale skin with roses on my cheeks, and little white teeth as delicate and even as a doll's. Edith, with a gap between her front teeth, envied my smile.

"All the makings of a desirable wife," my Aunt Ceci concluded whenever she saw me at holiday. "And so strong," she added when I carried the food platters to the table. She, like my mother, thought Edith put on airs that belonged anywhere but Montana, but they all agreed that, of the two of us, Edith had talent. I didn't mind; I was content to be thought pretty, and I knew how talented my sister was, how she could make something beautiful of the thinnest air.

"It's a work of art," I announced, fingering the pin curls around my face, admiring what I could see of the small, pink blossoms she'd woven into my braid.

"Thank you, Mrs. Berrian," she teased, tasting my new name in her mouth. I groaned and told her to go get ready. After she'd gathered her pink dress and bustled into the bathroom, I posed in front of the mirror, applying ice-pink lipstick and mouthing my name. *Hello, I'm Francine Berrian. Mrs. Berrian? That's me. I'm Mrs. Scott Berrian. Scott and Francine Berrian.* I might have run through the possibilities all morning if my mother hadn't stopped me.

"Enough of that foolishness," she snapped. "We're going to be late if your father doesn't find a car soon." She was wearing a cream-colored suit with matching pillbox hat that she'd borrowed from one of the church ladies. Mother was on the larger side, and I thought she looked like a lump of dough. Before I could find a kind way to suggest she go with her usual red church dress, I realized what she'd said.

"What do you mean '*find* a car'?" We had a car, a battered Chevy Bel-Air that my father had bought from one of his co-workers at the smelting plant. The guy had run it off the road while drunk, and because he didn't want to get his insurance cancelled, he'd sold it quick and cheap.

Mother sniffed and adjusted the button straining at her bosom. "It wouldn't start this morning. We were going to get donuts for breakfast, and it wouldn't start."

She shrugged and added that my father was visiting the neighbors to find someone who would help out. In those days just about anyone would lend a hand, so I stopped worrying and started hoping my father would scrounge up a shiny Thunderbird or something just as flashy. I'd heard of people who rented limousines to go to their weddings, but I wanted something that roared.

"You were going to get donuts?"

My mother always said she didn't believe in bakery products that weren't homemade. She said the sugar used by stores was bad for us, though we all knew the real issue was expense. "You've got a sweet tooth," she shrugged. "It's your wedding day."

Then she told me to hurry and finish dressing. I gladly obliged, eager to get to the chapel.

My parents were disappointed that we'd selected the air force base chapel instead of my home church. But we had to marry quickly, and the church was booked for many weekends to come. I was a bit disappointed myself, but I didn't let on around Scott or my mother. Pastor Redding had baptized me when I was a baby. He'd given me a white bible at my first communion, and his pocket was always full of butterscotch candies. It seemed only right that he marry me to my husband, but he was committed to the wedding of Sally Holmes and Allen Pettit, both remarrying after years of widowhood. Fortunately, most of the church members were coming to my wedding, including Pastor's wife. And they'd got Pastor's new assistant, Jonathan McEwen, to do the ceremony. It was his first wedding ever, but I wasn't worried. What could he screw up when everything was written down in a slender black book?

Edith helped me with the blue garter she'd given me, and after one last check in the mirror, we scurried to the kitchen to find our parents arguing. My father had a donut in his mouth. Powdered sugar snowed onto his suit jacket as he grunted in response to my mother's shrill chastisement.

"How could you forget to put gas in the car? Your own daughter's wedding. Were we all supposed to walk to the base?" She kept repeating the same questions as if she expected answers. My father shrugged and rolled his eyes at Marvin Kaplan, the neighbor who had apparently diagnosed the car's problem and taken my father for those donuts and a gallon of gasoline. I was relieved that the problem was solved and it wasn't me she was picking at, so I sneaked a chocolate-glazed donut from the white bakery box.

"Francine!" My mother shrieked. "You can't have chocolate. It'll make your face break out."

"In an hour's time?" I looked up at the kitchen clock, a German-made cuckoo clock that had belonged to my great-grandmother. It was nearly ten, and the wedding was set for eleven o'clock. Years later my own children would drive me crazy by shouting "I'm cuckoo for Cocoa Puffs!" every time this clock marked the hour, but then I liked the tinny ding and hollow "cuckoo!" that followed.

My mother had kept the clock hidden during the war because she was a patriot. After the war, patriotism then confirmed through the accumulation of material goods, she'd brought it out again, our only really valuable possession. It still worked beautifully, and as the eldest daughter, I was to inherit it. Now the ticking made me nervous, and the donuts didn't seem appetizing to my clenched stomach. Edith snatched the chocolate one from my hand and darted out onto the front step before anyone could complain.

My mother kept sniping at my father, and I surprised myself by calmly announcing, "There's no time for quibbling now. We need to get going." It sounded so adult, and my parents both stopped and considered me like I was a priestess delivering an oracle.

"Yes, Fred," my mother repeated, as though she were the one to pronounce our departure. "We need to get going."

He looked at Marvin, who shrugged and finished his cream-filled long john. My father looked like a gentleman in his Sunday suit, but I could tell from his expression that he wanted to impress his buddy and shock my mother by saying something slightly nasty. He glanced at me then, and his whole face seemed to open to absorb the image of his daughter as bride.

"But I don't want to get rid of her so soon." He mumbled that, then smiled shyly like he'd been forced into a confession. I was tickled. My father was usually more gruff with his children than my no-nonsense mother, more out of exhaustion than anything else. He worked long shifts at the smelter, and when he came home, his idea of relaxation was reorganizing his tools or, in winter, a hot bath and *Popular Mechanics*. He didn't want to be bothered.

I leaned in to hug him, but that was more than he could take in front of Marvin and my mother, so he patted my shoulder awkwardly and repeated that we'd best be going now that the Bel Air was "fixed."

We lived near downtown, and the fastest way to Malmstrom Air Force Base was also the scenic route that wrapped around the Missouri River and gave a view of the hydroelectric dams, the huge smokestack at the Anaconda Copper Company, and the rolling plains beyond. Pelicans in their arrow formation kept pace with the car as they glided over the water. The sky was a bright, vivid blue that morning as we drove silently, awed by the occasion. The only clouds were manmade, vapor trails that broke up and drifted into nothingness even as I watched.

I sometimes wished Scott were a flyboy instead of a missile technician. Flying seemed more glamorous to me, although my father, who liked Scott a great deal, defended him, saying that missiles would save us all from the communists. October's mess with the Cubans had us all scared, especially because Scott liked to brag that the Great Falls base would be one of Russia's first targets. "Don't worry," he said as he stroked the back of my neck. "We'll go up in a fiery ka-boom. No suffering in bomb shelters. Not in this part of the country."

I'd met him at a dance club and bar. This is not the story I told my parents, both of whom believed we met when my friend Sandy and I were eating ice cream at Gibson Park. I said we'd been eating and swapping gossip, and just as we started to crunch our cones, two handsome men had walked up and offered handkerchiefs for us to blot our sticky mouths. One was Sandy's boyfriend, Syl, and the other had been Scott. My mother loved this story, I could tell. She got a moony look in her eye whenever I told it, and then she'd ask my father why he didn't carry a handkerchief. This always got laughs because none of us could imagine Fred Linton with a handkerchief. He was a short, balding man with deep laugh lines around his eyes and permanent grease stains in the calluses of his hands. He might offer you a stick of gum but never a handkerchief.

I didn't have the heart to tell my mother that no one carried handkerchiefs anymore and certainly not in Montana. It was just a detail I added because it sounded romantic, and I'd seen it in picture shows. Once, when Scott had been over for dinner, my mother had just finished slicing onions for the meatloaf, and she came into the living room with a thin stream of tears on her cheek. She kept looking at Scott, repeating that she could use something to wipe her tears away. He was baffled, having never heard my detailed version of our supposed park encounter. When he pointed to her apron and suggested she use that, my mother whirled around in a huff, and at dinner she made him hint around and finally ask for second helpings.

Edith made fun of my handkerchief story, especially because she knew the real version. I'd been tipsy with beer at a bar and had literally fallen into Scott's lap. He and Syl were new to Great Falls, and Sandy and I recognized them as airmen right away from their flattops and formalities. We'd driven around the city for an hour or so, then gone to make out on Gore Hill, near the airport. Edith hated the handkerchief version because she said it was disgusting. "Eating ice cream cones and having two men, standing *over* you, give you something to wipe your creamy mouths with? Come on, Francie!" she squealed. Only my sister was allowed to call me that. There was a popular toy doll by that name, and I thought my full name was more sophisticated anyway. "Don't be vulgar," I'd told her, unsure of what exactly she was implying. Edith had a way with innuendo. Everything seemed sordid the way she said it. With my parents she was more careful, merely smart and sassy. With me, she verged on pornographic.

We were waved in without registering at the base gates because there was an air show open to the public that day. The poster advertised in capital letters: "ONE, TWO, THE BIG SKY BLUE: Watch 'em perform amazing air feats!!" My mother asked about the noise, and the MP assured us the show didn't start until noon, half an hour after the ceremony was to end. We drove on to the chapel, where a few cars waited in the parking lot. I recognized the family car of Sandy, who'd said she and Syl would arrive early to help out, and I recognized also the car of the organist, Mrs. Howe. My stomach was aching more from nerves or maybe the baby. I wasn't sure because my morning sickness came in the afternoons. At any rate, it roiled when my mother announced that Scott's car was nowhere to be seen.

"He's not supposed to be here yet, Mother," I said through tight lips. "It's bad luck to see the bride before the wedding, remember?" She'd told me that when he called the day before to ask if I could meet him for hamburgers. I'd turned him down, even though he said he really needed to see me. Edith said it would just build his anticipation anyway. "Same as holding out sex," she'd whispered. "He'll want you that much more."

"That doesn't mean he can't be here at a decent time," Mother snapped back. My father shot her a look that I didn't quite catch, and she turned and apologized. "He's a good boy. He'll be here soon, so we better get you inside." Edith rolled her eyes and held the car door open for me. I stepped out into a gust of wind that whipped my dress against my legs. Great Falls and all its wind. It's why we'd decided to braid my hair. A set would have gotten all tangled like my mother's. She took her hat off so the wind wouldn't, and immediately her curls tangled and frizzed.

"She forgot her kerchief," Edith giggled, making lip-smacking sounds. "Maybe Scott will have one for her." I slugged her, and we ran to the chapel, swinging the door open and startling Jonathan McEwen, who was scanning his prayer book. Others called him "Pastor," but I couldn't think of him that way. He seemed too young, so Edith and I referred to him as Jonathan, though never to his face. He'd only been with the church for three months, so we'd never had to talk to him before.

"Hi, Pastor," Edith greeted.

"Good morning," he replied, adopting a pastor's rich and theatrical tone of voice. Jonathan was six feet tall and skinny with a wild tangle of brown hair that he barely kept under control. He had small dark eyes, horn-rimmed glasses, and a long sloping nose that made him look scholarly. I knew he'd just graduated from a religious college somewhere back east. "It's a great day to be married," he offered, still looking at Edith.

It was the first time he'd met us. In those days people didn't do rehearsals and rehearsal dinners and all that. Edith was wearing light yellow, an increasingly popular color for brides who spat on tradition or, like myself, weren't allowed to wear white. So I could see why the young pastor thought she was the bride, but I still felt insulted. Didn't I have the glow of new life on me?

Edith pointed to me, and he repeated his statement about what a nice day it was. It seemed less and less nice to me as I stood in the formal chapel. Today I would meet my in-laws for the first time. They were flying in from Dallas so Mr. Berrian could stand as best man for his only son. I fretted that his mother wouldn't like me, and of course it would be too late. I'd be stuck for the rest of my life with people who hated me. But then I thought of Scott and the gentle way he had of stroking my hair and making me feel better, and I figured I could handle that for the rest of my life.

"I'd better get back to the little room before the guests arrive," I said. "Could you show us where it is?"

Jonathan walked us to a conference-style room with a full-length mirror on the door and said he'd come get us when the time came. Edith thanked him, and when he was gone, she whispered, "He's cute, don't you think?" I couldn't picture Edith with a pastor. I never imagined myself in that role—not then, I didn't.

We waited in the room together, making jokes and enduring my mother's constant checks. My father was seating guests, and my mother complained that he walked stiff as Frankenstein's monster. Sandy reported on who was there and who was not. At ten minutes to the ceremony, Scott and his family were still in the "not" category.

"Maybe they got held up at the airport," my mother suggested. "What time was he going to pick his folks up?"

"I don't know." I could hear my voice at a distance—hollow, robotic. I was scared and didn't know why, except I had a feeling I would never see Scott again. I imagined him driving too fast in his excitement. He'd run a red light or rear-end a farm pickup. The end.

"What do you mean you don't know?" My mother sounded irritated, but I recognized a sliver of panic that spiked my anxiety.

"You wouldn't let me talk to him yesterday!" It was the first and last time I ever shouted at my mother, and for effect I stamped my foot in a childish tantrum. The heel snapped off my right shoe. They were old shoes, so

I didn't feel guilty, just mortified that I'd be married in stocking feet, barefoot and pregnant in a holy sanctuary.

My father opened the door to the little waiting room, ready to take my arm and walk me down the chapel aisle. He seemed confused at first, but that quickly changed to anger. "You don't raise your voice to your mother!" he bellowed, his own voice elevating in volume with every word. I imagined the small knot of wedding guests pausing to listen. My mother must have, too, because she suddenly switched allegiances and told him I was just worried that Scott hadn't arrived. My father looked at his watch and seemed surprised that it really was eleven o'clock. He repeated that it was never okay to talk that way to a parent, but he lowered his voice.

Sometime in all this exchange my sister had slipped out. It was just the three of us in the waiting area: my parents and myself, dressed up again for a big event. The last one had been my high school graduation, only a week earlier. It seemed much, much longer since I'd stood with other nervous seniors in a too-long graduation gown borrowed from a neighbor's older son, straining to see my family and my almost-husband in the crowd. Neither of my parents had graduated high school, and they'd wanted to throw a party, but I asked them to save the celebration for my wedding, which was all that was on my mind as the class officers spoke of the future. No thoughts of the baby. Not then. I couldn't feel it or see it yet, and eighteen-year-olds need tangible evidence to believe. I think that's why they make lousy Christians. I couldn't build a future on the absence of monthly blood and an occasional wave of nausea, but Scott was real and solid under my fingers.

At two minutes past eleven, there was a brisk knock on the door, a knock that sounded a lot like Scott's. I jumped up from my chair and then insisted my mother answer, still thinking it bad luck to let him see me. My mother cracked the door. With a sigh, she swung it open to reveal Pastor Jonathan.

"Time to start," he said gently. "Where's the groom?"

My mother was quick to answer. "Just running a little late. Could you let the guests know?" Jonathan surveyed our faces, and we all gave him reassuring smiles that broke off as soon as he nodded and turned away. My father excused himself to the bathroom.

"I never said you couldn't call him," she defended herself. Her borrowed hat had slipped its bobby pins. It sat cocked on her head like a synthetic nest among brambles of hair.

"You did," I replied.

My voice was flat and lifeless, and I could feel a thickness in my muscles like I might fall over and sleep a hundred years. Like Rip Van Winkle, I'd wake and my mother would lay silent in her grave, no longer irritating me. My sister would be married with a host of adoring children and grandchildren crowning her golden years. My father? Well, he must have still been in the bathroom because I didn't have a place for him in my fantasy. Then there was me. Old and confused at 118. They'd find a bed in a nursing home, and they'd ask me to just go back to sleep. But after a hundred years' rest, I'd have insomnia. I'd probably die of it.

My father returned to find the situation unchanged. He stood awkwardly in his Sunday best with a vacant smile. Shortly after, Edith showed up, her face red and her eyes narrowed in barely restrained fury.

"Tell her," she demanded, stepping aside to reveal Syl, whose face was as red as Edith's. His head hung low. Sandy stood behind him, looking as confused as I felt. "Tell her!" My sister gave him a sharp push and he stumbled into the room. We all stared expectantly, hungry for an end to the waiting that seemed twice as long after eleven o'clock as it had before.

"He's gone," Syl explained, though it was no explanation.

"Gone where?" My mother and I asked at the same time, but he turned to me.

"Texas, I guess. I didn't think he'd really do it, Francine. I thought he was joking." Edith stood glaring at him, like Syl was the fugitive groom. I felt like I was in a dream, everything moving almost too slow, unreal.

Edith hastened our understanding. "Scott went to Texas to be with his girlfriend there. His family was never coming because they didn't know anything about you."

My father made a sound like a growl, and my mother put a hand on my shoulder. I wanted to fall in her arms and bawl like a baby.

"He had another girl? And you never told us?" Sandy lit into Syl. Later they would break up over my failed wedding, and that night at the bar with the flyboys would be as if it had never happened. Sandy said she couldn't trust him after that, and she kept imagining a farm girl back in Wisconsin, pining for him to come home.

My father was the one who stepped up. He went and spoke to the guests, sending each home with whatever they'd brought and an apology. He took down the plastic flower wreaths that Edith had arranged for the chapel, and he called the grocer, who'd made a small wedding cake, and said we didn't need it. It was pre-paid though, so he picked it up the next morning and took it to church for social time after the service. I didn't mind. I never wanted to see, smell, or taste it. Edith told me later that it was too sweet.

I think my mother was in shock. She spoke very little and kept trying to touch me, her way of commiserating and apologizing for all the bickering the wedding had caused between us. She told me to stay home from church the next day, to rest my eyes, which by then would be sorely puffed from crying. Finally, standing in the waiting room, no longer waiting, I asked her to give me time alone, and she disappeared without a peep, probably to talk to my Aunt Ceci, who'd taken a bus from Butte to get here.

In my stocking feet, I slipped out the back door because I wasn't ready for the sympathy pats and the pitying looks. Let my sister handle that—she'd rip into Scott Berrian until they'd be afraid to mention his name at all. The pavement was cool and solid under my feet. The wind had trickled to a light breeze, unusually warm for early summer in Montana. It played with the curls around my cheeks, and when I closed my eyes, I imagined it was Scott's breath the first night he made love to me. I'm still ashamed that I yielded so easily, but it was so sweet, despite my fear that Scott's roommate would walk in, despite the strange sensations and pressure in places I'd never felt before.

A year later, Edith called me, crying and convinced she was bleeding to death. I could hear a man's voice in the background repeating "Oh Jesus" in high, frightened tones. I'd nearly hung up to call the police, but I realized it was only her hymen that had broken. Explaining that, I saw how she knew much less than I'd thought.

So my first experience, even if it convinced me to marry or burn in hell, was a good one. I was standing in back of that chapel, remembering the best of my former husband-to-be, not the fact that he'd gone AWOL from me and his career. I never did hear what happened to him for abandoning his post. I wasn't interested in the end of his story. I was remembering Scott, shirtless and leaning over me, the radio playing the Four Seasons, my body shivering from fear and anticipation. Eyes closed against the increasing wind, I hummed to my memory of "Big Girls Don't Cry" and was startled by a hand on my shoulder.

In a fairy tale, the hand would have belonged to Scott Berrian. He would have realized his cowardice and hurried back to marry me. But it was Pastor Jonathan who stood at my side. I braced myself for his sympathy or, worse, the platitude about this all being a part of God's plan. Right then I needed only to remain in Scott's ghostly embrace, but Jonathan snapped that spell. He dropped his hand and pointed over my left shoulder.

"Look," he said. "The air show." Sure enough, six jets were storming to heaven in close formation. I had been so lost in my dreams I had barely noticed the racket they made. The jets splintered out of formation and began to loop in and out of each other's paths. The choreography was amazing, the danger thrilling. The thunder of the jet engines overhead drowned out everything—the crowd's roar of applause at each stunt, the whine of the wind, Jonathan's small talk about how he'd loved airplanes since he was a little kid.

I made him repeat himself when the jets strayed far enough out to make conversation possible. He said, "I wanted to be a flyboy, but I found safer ways to be near God." He grinned, and I could see the little boy he'd been, the eager child who'd held toy planes in his outstretched hands and dreamed of flying. I smiled back, my way of assuring him that his dream was great, its loss no more than what was to be expected. I ignored the sting of tears at the back of my throat, my mouth spread as wide and carefree as possible.

"Safer ways," I repeated, watching the jets shredding the air, their wingtips almost seeming to touch.

That Christmas, after the baby that was never much of a baby slipped away in a clot of blood, after four months of working the phones at the oil refinery and avoiding the men who brushed their hands against me, I quit my job, and I married my pastor. My mother said nothing about my lily-white dress.

Six years later, well-versed in Jonathan's faith and pregnant with our second child, I watched Neil Armstrong take his magical step. My small son, sitting on his father's lap, clapped his hands wildly, and like most mothers that year, I imagined him becoming an astronaut.

As I watched Neil bounce so lightly on the surface of that pitted moon, I felt my child kick. The movement sent a small, deep shiver through me, and I thought of Scott for the first time in a long while. My body's memory flashed sharp. Sensations I'd never known with Jonathan soared through my muscles in a long, hard ache. Tears tickled my eyelashes, and when my husband saw my face, he smiled. "Amazing, isn't it?"

I nodded.

I couldn't sleep that night, so I got up and wandered into my son's room, bumping my head on the little mobile above him: circus animals wearing funny hats. I brushed a sweaty strand of hair from his brow and put my lips close to his ear.

"Fly," I whispered. "Fly, fly, fly."

Chauna Craig has published her stories and essays in numerous anthologies and literary journals, including *Ploughshares*, *Prairie Schooner*, *Fourth Genre*, and *Sou'wester*. She's been awarded fellowships and scholarships to Vermont Studio Center, Hedgebrook, and Bread Loaf Writer's Conference. A Montana native, she currently lives in western Pennsylvania.

The Widow's Guide to Edible Mushrooms was her debut story collection, and *Wings & Other Things* is her second, with Press 53.

ACKNOWLEDGMENTS

Thank you to the editors of the magazines and anthologies where some of these stories first appeared, including Allison Joseph, Jessica Cory, Morgan Beatty, Ladette Randolph, Rose Huber Kelly, and Tara Laskowski. Also, deep appreciation to Hedgebrook, where I drafted some of these stories, and to Minal Hajratwala and the Unicorn Club, for nurturing and writerly support in a pandemic.

To Claire Foxx for outstanding editing and a groovy book cover, and to Kevin Morgan Watson, in deep appreciation for your long commitment to independent publishing.

To early reader Atalie Soule for your reflections on these stories, especially these observations: "the author of this collection is quirky and weird" and "don't we sometimes see the way out, that postage stamp of sky, but we continue to flap around aimlessly in the darkness?" Yes. And good grief, yes.

While I'm lucky to have an excellent support system in all areas of life, a special shout-out to the people who most directly helped with aspects of this book: John Yu Branscum and Izzy Yu, Sherrie Flick, and the writers who agreed to preview and write blurbs for this collection: Geeta Kothari, Donna Miscolta, Kerry Neville, and Michelle Ross.

And finally, to those who create the joyful home to which I always want to return: Wyn, Zo, and Dave. I am so grateful for you all.